A splash and a the main house.

He ran toward the pond as Claire surfaced, spluttering and laughing.

"Come on in."

He gave her his best "you've got to be kidding me" look.

Laughing, she splashed him. "It's just a little cold water."

Joe took a deep breath and dived in, surfacing beside her.

"Are you worried about the meeting?" he asked when his breath had regulated.

"Yes."

"Don't give up. I don't know if you're that good with all kids, but if it wasn't for you, Amelia and I would still be deadlocked in the silent treatment."

She smiled. "Thank you. I needed the reminder of why it's so important."

"I have the feeling that you're too stubborn to give up, anyway."

"Oh, you do know how to sweet-talk me, Joe Sheehan." She clambered out of the pond.

As he watched her, he realized he really liked her and he hadn't felt that way about someone in a long time. The doors to his heart had been firmly closed. Seemed now there was just a crack in the door, enough to think…maybe.

Award-winning author **Stephanie Dees** lives
in small-town Alabama with her pastor husband
and two youngest children. A Southern girl
through and through, she loves sweet tea,
SEC football, corn on the cob and air-conditioning.
For further information, please visit her website
at stephaniedees.com.

Books by Stephanie Dees

Love Inspired

Family Blessings
The Dad Next Door

The Dad Next Door

Stephanie Dees

HARLEQUIN® LOVE INSPIRED®

Recycling programs for this product may not exist in your area.

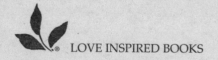

LOVE INSPIRED BOOKS

ISBN-13: 978-0-373-89931-9

The Dad Next Door

Copyright © 2017 by Stephanie Newton

www.Harlequin.com

Printed in U.S.A.

Yet still I dare to hope when I remember this:
The faithful love of the Lord never ends!
His mercies never cease. Great is His faithfulness;
His mercies begin afresh each morning.
—Lamentations 3:21–23

For Melissa Endlich and Melissa Jeglinski
Thanks for keeping the faith.

Chapter One

Claire Conley stood on the overgrown lawn—the Alabama humidity wilting her hair, flies circling—as she confronted her legacy. The antebellum plantation house she'd inherited from her father looked nothing like the pictures the lawyer had sent her. Well, to be fair, there was a porch. And it did have huge columns. But that was where the similarity ended. What had looked like pristine white paint in the photo was gray and peeling. The yard was a tangle of weeds.

Tears stung in her eyes. She'd sold everything she owned and driven fourteen hours on coffee and adrenaline, dreams buzzing in her head. For this?

This worn-out, falling-down piece of… history?

She tried to push the long, shaking sob back

to where it came from and failed. She didn't know what she'd been hoping. Her biological father had never given her a thing. This was just more of the same.

She didn't hear the truck coming up the drive until the door slammed behind her. She spun around.

He looked hard. Hard muscles, hard expression, head shaved military style, a shadow of stubble along his jaw. A hint of a dimple creased his face, but she couldn't see his eyes.

Those were covered with silver aviator glasses.

She was suddenly, painfully, aware of the fact that she'd chosen to stay on the road instead of stopping to eat in Somewhere, Georgia, and had the evidence of it smeared on her comfiest—threadbare—jeans.

"I'm looking for Claire Conley." He didn't raise his voice, but still, it carried.

She nodded, not sure she could speak around the lump in her throat. "That would be me."

"I'm Joe Sheehan." The guy walked closer and dug into his jeans pocket, coming up with a key. "Your father's attorney asked me to give this to you. He's out of town for a few weeks."

She narrowed her eyes, big-city self-preservation kicking in. "You local law enforcement?"

"I'm a cop, but not in Red Hill Springs. My

mom owns the diner and the attorney asked me to meet you."

"You sure he didn't skip town because he was afraid to face me?"

"I'm sorry?" The hand holding the key dropped a bit and the look on his face changed from friendly to concerned. "Is everything okay?"

She took a deep breath through her nose and let it out. The internet told her cleansing breaths were supposed to be calming. Not so much. "Yes, it's fine. I'm fine. I was just expecting the house to be in a little better condition. I'm opening…I have plans for this place."

Joe looked skeptical. "Yeah? Bed-and-breakfast?"

"Kind of. You know, my pastor back in North Carolina tells me brokenness is a good thing." She stared at the house, her voice trailing off. If that was true, she was golden. She'd been wrecked when her fiancé ditched her, but thought she could get past it. Her mother's death from cancer had gutted her. And when her job with the county ended, she figured God was trying to tell her something.

Joe rubbed his shoulder. "I'm not sure about it being a good thing, but I think things that are broken can be fixed. At least I hope so."

Maybe he was right. Maybe this old place

could be renovated. She didn't know if there was enough glue in the world to hold her life together, but she was going to give it a try. Her hard-won optimism resurfaced, at least briefly.

Claire mentally calculated what remained in her bank account, and...the moment of optimism was gone. "I don't know if I can do this. I have six months of living expenses and what's left of my mom's life insurance to get this place running."

Joe stepped closer. "Maybe you should go inside?"

She closed her eyes, realizing she'd been spilling her guts to a literal stranger. And why? Because she got the sense that he understood what rebuilding a home—a life—would cost her?

"I've heard it was a real showplace at one time." Joe climbed the steps to the porch.

"That's encouraging." She followed him onto the wide porch and took a step forward. Her left foot went right through the wood plank.

Joe's arm streaked out to wrap around her waist, keeping her from falling through. He was warm and solid and, just for a second, she wanted to lean into that warmth. Instead, a laugh bubbled to the surface. And then the rest of it billowed out.

He hauled her to her feet and she stared at her reflection in those silver sunglasses. Hair all wackadoo, no lipstick, a ketchup stain on her shirt. Another giggle rose to the surface and she shoved it back with a tiny little snort. "Sorry."

"No problem." Joe slid the key in the lock. Despite the general disrepair, the key turned easily. He pushed the door open and stepped aside so she could go first.

It was like stepping into another time. The front hall had high ceilings, to combat the summer heat, and though the wallpaper was peeling, she could see that it would've been beautiful in its day. French doors to her right opened into a huge room, floor-to-ceiling windows sending long squares of golden light onto the wood floor. "What would this room have been used for?"

"I think it was the ballroom. The mayor and his wife had dinner parties here." At her side, Joe pulled off the sunglasses, sliding them into his shirt pocket. There was an ugly, twisted scar streaking from the corner of his eye into his hairline.

She swallowed a gasp as he turned toward her, catching her staring. "Your eyes are blue," she blurted.

"So are yours."

"Right. Of course they are."

Amusement deepened the dimple in his cheek and she glanced wildly around for a change of topic. "I can just see it, the room filled with tables covered in crisp white linen, sparkling crystal, heavy silver. What kind of food did they serve, do you think?"

Joe stepped farther into the room, a glint of humor in his eyes. "I'm not quite old enough to have come to the parties, but my mom told me about them. I think the governor was here a time or two."

She nodded, turning slowly in the room, hearing the music that had once played. What would her life have been like if she'd grown up here with her biological family? Would she have had pretend parties with her friends in this grand room? Even thinking it made her feel guilty, like she was cheating on her real family, the family that raised her. But one day children would run and play, spin and twirl, in this room.

She turned back to him. "How in the world did they live in this place with it in this kind of shape?"

Joe's brows drew together. "They didn't. From what I understand, they moved to a house in town about ten years ago."

Well, that explained a lot. And yet, there

was something here, some sense of the past that was captivating. There were several rooms opening off to the right of the large hall, a parlor-type room, bedroom, bathroom. "Do you know where the kitchen is?"

"It runs along the back of the house. It used to be outside, but Mrs. Carter had one built inside the year she moved in."

"Wait. The kitchen was still behind the house when the former mayor got married?"

"Yes, too hot in the South back in the day to have the kitchen inside." Joe led the way to the back of the house. "Why do you call him the mayor and not your father?"

The dim corridor was cool, almost chilly, despite the heat outside, the humid air soft on her skin. "He was only my biological father. I didn't know him. My twin sister and I were adopted by another family."

She walked into the kitchen and stared hopelessly at the peeling linoleum and kitchen cabinets, which were painted a color that might have been fashionable about thirty years ago. All hint of laughter vanished. There was so much work to do if she was going to make this sagging place into any kind of home. She tried the deep breath thing again, and again it clogged in her throat.

Behind her, he said, "I'm sorry."

"About my father?" She shrugged. "It's okay. I didn't know him. And I had a great mom. One good parent is better than two bad ones."

"You think so?" He locked eyes with her, the blue of his startlingly clear in the shadowy room.

"Of course." She looked away. That she didn't need a father was something she'd told herself all through her growing-up years. The real truth was somewhere in the middle. There was a hole where a father should've been, yeah, but nothing compared to the gaping cavern of not having parents at all.

The one visit she and her twin sister, Jordan, had with their birth father had left her with more questions than answers about who she was. Her birth mother had died shortly after giving birth. Their dad didn't feel like he could raise infant twin girls on his own, so he'd put them both up for adoption.

She looked back at Joe. "Kids need a constant in their life. Just showing up is half the battle."

"I hope you're right." Joe pulled his phone out of his back pocket and looked at the screen. "Listen, I have to go. My daughter, Amelia, is going to be waiting for me at the school. If I don't get there on time…well, let's just say I need to show up."

She smiled. "Thank you for bringing the key by. I'm sorry if I seem a little distracted. Being a homeowner is new to me."

"No problem," he said again. "Do you need anything?"

"No, thanks." Her eyes filled—the traitorous truth that she did need. So much. Too much. She needed connection and roots. To build something lasting, to somehow fill the void that her mom had left, and the one that had always been where her father should have been.

No one could help her with that, not even a handsome stranger with kind blue eyes. Okay, yeah, she'd noticed he was handsome, but she wasn't interested. She'd done love and gotten her heart stomped on. And she definitely didn't have time for casual. So, no, thanks.

"Okay, if you're sure." He slid the aviators back over his eyes, then pulled a somewhat tattered business card out of his wallet. "It's old, but the cell number's still good. Feel free to call me if you think of anything."

Claire glanced at the soft-edged card. "Full-service operation you're running here."

"Always aim to please." He smiled for the first time, and despite her earlier lecture to herself, her heart gave a silly little skip. "Welcome to Red Hill Springs, Claire."

His footsteps echoed in the empty house as

he left. She followed and watched from the front door as he drove his old F-150 down the drive. When he turned onto the highway, she looked up.

What she could see of the sky through the overgrown bushes was crystal clear and a shade of blue she'd never seen in the city. *Are you there, God? Because I really need You to show up.*

She hesitated, then looked back at the sky. *Like, now.*

Maybe God didn't like being given a time-line, she didn't know, but maybe He would understand that she had one. This place had to be up and running and making ends meet within six months, or she was toast. And not the good kind of toast, either. The burned kind that made your house smell bad and no one would eat, even if you scraped off the top layer.

Turning back to the house, she sighed and reached for the light switch. Nothing happened.

"Oh, perfect." She closed her eyes. "Just… perfect."

"The café was buzzing today about the mayor's daughter turning the plantation house into a bed-and-breakfast. She filed a permit for renovation last week before she ever set eyes on the place." Joe's mom tasted the lima beans and turned the heat off on the stove.

"Is that so?" Joe washed his hands at the sink in his mother's kitchen.

Her eyes sparkled with suppressed laughter. "Yes. I think it's about as bad as the time Hester Jenkins set John's Dale Earnhardt collection on fire on their front lawn."

He shot his mom a glance. "I wouldn't know about that."

"Oh, that's right. You were somewhere in the sand when that happened."

Somewhere in the sand. His mother's way of making her son's military deployment bearable. Somewhere in the sand sounded like he could be on a tropical beach smoothing on sunscreen. Not in the middle of a war zone being shot at.

"John dropped the charges the next week, right after he broke her grandmother's Lladro figurine, by accident, of course. It's not a police matter anymore."

"Glad to hear it." His voice was wry and his mother made a face at him.

"Spoilsport. What's the mayor's daughter like? I'd like to get a look at her."

"I'm sure you'll meet her soon enough. Everyone comes into the Hilltop eventually." He sifted through his thoughts about the newest resident of Red Hill Springs. "She's pretty. Dark brown hair, blue eyes. Five-three or four."

"Once a cop always a cop. Sounds like you could pick her out in a lineup."

He caught the sassy sarcasm and ignored it, instead choosing to appease his mother's innate curiosity. "She seemed…I don't know, lost? But also determined to make a go of that old place." He tossed his keys into a tray on the counter, where his father had tossed his, along with his badge, for as long as Joe could remember. And then there was a pang, because Frank was gone. A heart attack had taken him from them with no warning a year ago next month.

Joe had been seven the first time he'd sworn he was leaving this town and never coming back. Eight when he'd stopped hoping his parents could be trusted. Twelve when he'd gotten caught trying to break into the police chief's garage.

So yeah, he knew a little bit about being lost. He'd been an angry, defensive kid, striking out at everyone and trusting no one, but instead of arresting him, Frank had taken him inside to Bertie and Bertie had taken him under her wing. Slowly, he'd realized there were no more bruises, no more wondering when he would get to eat again, no more being scared every single minute of every day.

They'd rescued him from that life, even though they wouldn't say so, and then they'd adopted him, giving him a real mom and dad, a brother, two sisters and a life he'd never expected. He wasn't sure he'd ever get over the feeling of stepping into someone else's life, wondering when they would realize he didn't belong.

Bertie tossed some cherry tomatoes into the salad bowl. "Maybe she's a little like Amelia, in a way, not having a daddy growing up? I think Amelia feels a little lost, too."

And there it was, what his mother really wanted to get at. The very new relationship between him and his daughter. "Amelia has a daddy. Unfortunately, her mother—and believe me, I use that term loosely—was the only one who knew it."

He heard a noise behind him, a small rush of air, and turned to see his daughter, Amelia. Just her back and a whirl of dark brown hair as she stormed out of the room, slamming the door behind her. Joe stared at the closed door, the perfect metaphor for their relationship. "She wasn't at school today when I got there. She walked home alone again."

He felt his mother's hand on his back. "She'll come around, bud. She's had a lot of change to deal with. All that anger hides how she really feels."

"She hasn't spoken a word to me in the two weeks that she's been here." He had a lot of ground to make up with Amelia, he knew that. He may not be ready to be a dad, but he was one, and he didn't want to screw it up. But where in the world did you start when you'd missed twelve years?

"Joe, she was dropped off at the door with a note and a backpack full of clothes that didn't fit her. Give her some time. You weren't exactly a bundle of joy when you first came here."

That was an accurate statement. He paused for a second. "Did you ever regret it, taking me on?"

She shut the refrigerator door and grabbed his face between her hands, like she used to do when he was younger. "Darling boy, I would never regret you. You are *my* son in every way that counts. It's tricky now, but soon you'll be finding your way. I promise."

Fighting the knot in his throat, he said, "I would do anything to be able to go back and make it right for her."

After high school, he'd gone straight into basic training. He'd been in Afghanistan when Lori Ann was having his baby. She could've gotten word to him, but she didn't try. He had no idea Amelia even existed until she showed up on his mom's doorstep and he'd seen his own blue eyes staring up at him.

"I know you would do anything for her, and one day Amelia will understand that, too." Constantly moving, she stirred the okra and tapped the wooden spoon on the side of the pan. "It's normal, Joe, to have feelings and questions about your childhood. You've had a rough few months. It's no wonder you have questions."

Maybe that was what brought Claire to Red Hill Springs, the questions that she'd never had the answers to.

"How long did you stay out there at the plantation? Was she nice?"

Long used to his mother's seeming ability to mind-read, Joe shrugged, but he remembered the look on Claire's face as she'd stared at her inheritance. "Her name is Claire. She seemed nice enough. A little thrown by the condition of the place. It's falling down."

"Is she staying at a hotel in Spanish Fort?"

"No, I think she's staying there at the plantation."

"That place is a dump." Bertie pointed the spoon his way. He watched it warily as he sneaked a taste of the limas from the edge of the pan closest to him. "Go pick her up for dinner and tell her to bring her stuff. She can sleep in Wynn's room."

"Mom, I'm not sure that's a good idea." He rubbed his shoulder, sending a sidelong glance at the firmly closed door to the living room. "We have a lot going on right now."

"We do." His mother nodded in agreement. "But no one should show up in town and be left without a hot meal or a clean place to lay her head."

He didn't want to get involved. He wasn't like his mother. Trusting, having faith, it didn't come easily to him. A wary sense of self-preservation had been ingrained in him as a kid. Then he fought a war on foreign soil. And then he became a cop.

But he picked up his keys and said, "You're sure about this?"

"Do I look undecided?" His mom had blond hair cut into a straight bob at her chin. She always looked perfectly groomed, even standing over a hot stove, or after a long day on her feet in the café. What she didn't look was indecisive.

Arguing with his mother was pointless. Once Bertie took on a project, the best thing to do was get out of the way. Even his father could never say no to her, which was how they ended up with two cats, four dogs and an extra kid.

Now she was wanting to take in the mayor's daughter, and that was the last thing he needed.

Chapter Two

Claire leaned over the kitchen table, her pen moving almost as fast as her mind as she made an action list for the next day. A small mountain of chocolate wrappers smushed into little silver balls lined the table. The shock had faded and been replaced by a certainty that no matter how hard this was, she wasn't going to back down. Of course, electricity would help.

The house was completely dark now except for the kitchen, which was lit by the several dozen candles she'd found in the closets around the house. A large room that ran the width of the house with a fireplace at one end, the kitchen had real potential as a gathering place.

At current count, there were one hundred and forty-two things on the to-do list and that was just for the house. It didn't begin to cover the mountain of paperwork and red tape she had to tackle.

A knock at the open door was loud in the too-quiet house. She jumped to her feet, her hand at her chest. Through the screen, she saw the guy from earlier.

Joe, he'd said his name was. He was still dressed the same, except for the boots, which she hadn't noticed before. They were scuffed and dusty and well-worn, which made her think there might be some hope for him. He didn't have the sunglasses on, but they were in his T-shirt pocket.

"Sorry, I didn't mean to startle you. You were pretty deep in thought." He gave her a little apologetic shrug.

She walked to the door. "I didn't expect to see you again so soon. Is there a problem?"

He shook his head. "No, not at all. You look busy."

She'd changed into different jeans —ones without a stain—and a soft, loose T-shirt. Not so fancy, but at least it was clean. "I'm making a list. A very long list."

"May I come in?"

She hesitated before she unlatched the screen, but it wasn't like he hadn't been alone with her in the house this afternoon and this wasn't the big city. People were probably neighborly here. She pushed the door open and he stepped inside the room. "I have a few Diet Cokes left in my cooler if you'd like one."

"No, thanks, I'm good." He tested a chair before he sat down in it. "What's first on the list?"

"Getting more candles. Or even better, electricity."

The corner of his mouth kicked up again. "That does seem like a priority."

"Right?" She stacked the papers on the table and watched as the shadows from the candles danced across his face. "Before it got dark, I was able to look around a little bit. Most of the house is structurally sound, but all of it needs work if it's going to be livable."

"It sounds like a huge undertaking."

She appreciated that he didn't try to sugar-coat the truth. It *was* a huge undertaking. Gigantic. She blinked. "Yeah. My mom wasn't afraid of picking up a hammer and taught me to be the same way, so I can do some of the work myself, but even so, the timetable is going to be tight."

"It's a beautiful old place. It will be great when it's all fixed up." His eyes were gentle and hers stung, again.

She told herself to get a grip. "Thanks. I

think it can be, too. So what brings you out this way again?"

Joe cleared his throat. "My mom always cooks enough food for the entire block and she wanted me to invite you to dinner. It's also possible that she wants to get a good look at you before the rest of the town does."

"That's nice...I think." The candles flickered in the breeze from the open window and she glanced around the dim room. "You live with your mom?"

A bark of laughter escaped. "Yes, thanks for mentioning that. I wasn't planning on staying in Red Hill Springs long enough to need my own place. My daughter is living with me now, though, so I'm looking. It's hard to find a short-term rental in a town this size."

"What brought you back to Red Hill Springs?"

"My dad died. I got shot." He shrugged, like that kind of thing happened every day.

"Were you hurt badly? How long are you in town for? How old is your daughter?" So many questions. He was so much less predictable than she'd thought when she first met him. Those boots didn't lie.

"I was shot in the line of duty. I'm a cop, like my dad was. I've been here for four months rehabbing my shoulder and will be here at least two more. And Amelia's twelve."

She was quiet for a moment, absorbing all the information. "Does your daughter like it here?"

Joe grimaced. "I wouldn't normally lead with this information, but if you're around town at all, you'll hear it. Her mother—" He stumbled a little on that word but quickly recovered. "Her mother decided to go into rehab and dropped her off at my mom's with a note and a backpack. I didn't know she existed."

Dark lashes had dropped over his eyes and she couldn't see his expression. But the tone of his voice sounded like shame and that wasn't okay. "Rehab is good, I guess, right?"

"If that's where she actually went. I've checked all the ones within a few hours' drive and she isn't registered at any of them. She made a bad mistake, but I'm not sorry my daughter is with me." He made a face. "Amelia's not too happy about it, but that's another story."

Claire didn't know why she felt such a kinship with this man she didn't know, but there was something. Maybe it was that he was starting his life over with a daughter and she was starting over, period.

Maybe.

She looked at him, considered. And then thought, why not? "There's a little cabin on the property, on the other side of the pond from here. It's in pretty bad shape from what I can tell, but if you want to look at it tomorrow, you're welcome to it."

His head snapped up. "How much do you want for rent?"

"We can talk about the rent after you see it. It's not much, but it has a pretty view."

"I really don't know how long I'll be here, but thank you, it's a kind offer." He stood. "We should be getting back for dinner. And I forgot to mention my mom also said to tell you to bring your bag and you can sleep in my sister's room."

The thought of not spending the night on the floor in this creepy, silent house was appealing, but she didn't move. "That's really not necessary. I don't want to put your mother out."

"You won't be putting her out, believe me. Plus, she insisted and I'll get in trouble if you don't."

The thought of this big, muscular man getting in trouble with his mom amused her. "I do appreciate it, but this is going to be my home. I think I better get used to it."

In the distance, an animal howled. The haunting sound hung in the air. Claire's heart began to pound. "What was that?"

"Sounded like a coyote. They're opportunistic hunters, but you're probably fine in here."

She couldn't really see his expression across the room in the candlelight, but he seemed dead serious. Maybe she should go to stay at his mother's house.

No. Maybe it was pure stubbornness, but she was staying. "I'll be fine. Please tell your mom I appreciate the offer and I'll look forward to meeting her."

He looked skeptical but didn't argue. "If you're sure."

She wasn't sure at all. "I am."

"Okay, then, I'll see you around." He swung the screen door open and a few minutes later, all she could see was the taillights of his truck headed away from her house.

The coyote howled again, and this time he was joined by his friends. She closed the door and locked it. It was going to be a long night.

Joe lifted the cup of coffee and savored a moment of peace before the battle began again. The battle for ground with Amelia, the battle to rehab his shoulder and regain his range of motion. He clenched his fist and uncurled his fingers one at a time.

In the kitchen, pans clanged, bacon sizzled and Martin, the cook, yelled, "Order up." His mother bustled behind the counter, a ready smile and a fresh cup of coffee for everyone.

Behind the silver aviators, he watched his twelve-year-old daughter across the Formica table from him. Her eyes were on her cell phone, thumbs flying. She might as well have been in another state for all the attention she was paying him. "What do you want for breakfast, Amelia?"

She didn't look up.

Lanna, best waitress at the Hilltop, stopped at their table. "Hey, Joe, what'll it be?"

They'd been friends since middle school when they used to sneak behind the gym for a smoke. She'd written him letters every single month while he'd been overseas. "I'll have my usual and Amelia will have blueberry pancakes."

Lanna topped off his coffee from the pot on her tray and raised one perfectly arched eyebrow. "Pancakes today. All right, then. Be back in a jiff."

Every day Joe insisted that Amelia join him for breakfast before school at his mother's diner. Every day she refused to eat. Every day he ordered her something different off the menu, figuring eventually he'd order something she wouldn't be able to refuse.

"How's school going? Have you gotten to know any of your teachers?"

No answer.

"My favorite teacher was Mr. McAdams. We called him the Mac Attack. He brought doughnuts to our homeroom every Friday." He looked up as Lanna brought their food and slid it onto the table, along with a warm pitcher of maple syrup.

"There you go. Y'all holler if you need anything, okay? Bertie said to tell you she put extra blueberries in the pancakes, just for you, Amelia."

Amelia still didn't look up, but he saw her swallow hard. The edges of the pancakes were crisp and buttery, the scent of blueberries and warm maple syrup mingling in the air. It had to be getting to her.

The chimes at the entrance jingled and Claire Conley came through the door, light brown ponytail swinging. She had jeans and a sweatshirt on, but as she got closer, he saw the edge of a flannel pajama top sticking out from under the sweatshirt. There was a crease in her cheek from a pillow. She obviously needed coffee more than he did. As she caught sight of him, he held a mug up to her, an offering.

Claire cupped it in both hands and took a long, greedy sip, sighing in appreciation.

"Thanks. Obviously, I didn't think this through. No electricity means no coffee. And I didn't get to sleep until about four. Crazy coyotes."

"Claire Conley, this is my daughter, Amelia."

Amelia still didn't speak, but she did look up to check Claire out.

Claire smiled at her, seemingly oblivious to the tension between the two of them. "I just came in to pick up some breakfast. I have to get back to the farm. My horse is being trailered in today. Amelia, you'll have to come and see him."

Amelia's blue eyes widened. "Is she pretty?"

"Yes, very handsome. His name is Freckles." Claire dug her cell phone out of her back pocket and showed Amelia a picture.

"He's awesome. I want to be a vet one day."

Joe looked from Amelia to Claire. Amelia had just said more words in the last sixty seconds than Joe had heard in two weeks. He jumped into the conversation. "I'll pick you up after school and we'll go see Claire's horse, if you want."

She shot him a quelling look, grabbed her phone and shrugged into her backpack at the faint sound of a bell ringing in the distance. "It's time for school. See you later, Claire."

Watching as she crossed the street to the

school, Joe couldn't help but think she looked so small with that enormous backpack. He turned back to Claire. "I can't believe you got her to talk. She's been on a conversation strike."

She shrugged and he waved at the bench across from him. "Feel free to eat the pancakes. She didn't touch them. She's on an eating strike, too."

Sliding onto the red vinyl bench across from him, Claire looked up, startled. "She's not eating? For how long?"

"Don't worry, she eats. Just not with me. She doesn't trust me and, really, I don't blame her. She thought I didn't want anything to do with her for twelve years."

Lanna slid a to-go box onto the table in front of Joe. "For the pancakes. Coffee for you, miss?"

"Claire Conley. It's nice to meet you. I'd love some coffee, thanks."

"Claire…got it. I'm Lanna." The light dawned in Lanna's eyes as she poured a mug for Claire and placed some cream on the table. "You're the mayor's daughter. No one even knew the mayor had a daughter. Everyone's talking about it. Need anything else, just yell."

"It was a closed adoption, so I didn't know the mayor was my father, either, until recently.

I guess my arrival will be fueling the town gossip for a while." Claire's eyes sparkled with amusement as Lanna hustled back to the kitchen.

"No worries. Pretty sure Amelia and I still occupy the top spot." Joe cleared his throat. "So, the coyotes kept you awake?"

"I didn't even know coyotes were a thing, but I looked it up on the internet on my phone. There are hordes of them." She shuddered. "But they're afraid of donkeys, so guess who will be getting a couple as soon as the funds allow?" Claire grinned and shoved a huge bite of blueberry pancakes into her mouth.

"I'm guessing that would be you."

"These are so good." She took another big bite out of the pancakes and picked up her mug. "Okay, so when you come out to the farm to look at the cabin later on, bring Amelia to see Freckles. He really is good with kids."

"Believe it or not, that exit this morning was progress. The first week, she wasn't nearly as friendly and affectionate."

She laughed and almost choked on her coffee. "I know you probably keep hearing this, but give it some time, you're doing fine."

Joe narrowed his eyes at her. "And you know this because you have a bunch of teenage daughters who hate you, so you've been through the process?"

Claire laughed again, her lake-blue eyes wide-open now. "Something like that. I'm a social worker. I had a bunch of teenagers in my caseload who hated my guts and a few younger kids who could give them a run for their money. I loved the feeling when they eventually learned they could trust me. And you will, too, once you get past this stage."

"How exactly do I do that?"

"By doing what you're doing. Don't let her get away with not sitting at the table or join-ing in family outings. The daily breakfasts are good. Eventually, she'll get the idea that you're sticking."

He studied her face as she talked—ani-mated, alive—and comprehension dawned. He had enough instincts and experience to see trouble brewing. "So when you say you're 'kind of' opening a bed-and-breakfast, what you really mean is you're turning your inheri-tance into a foster home, where kids will have a bed and eat breakfast."

She had the grace to blush. "Yes, something like that."

"Were you trying to hide the truth?" He wasn't opposed to giving her the benefit of the doubt, but this new friendship might be short-lived if she had a habit of lying.

"No! Really, I wasn't. You assumed bed-and-breakfast and I didn't correct you. I never intended to keep it a secret."

"A foster home is going to raise some eyebrows in this town." Not that he cared. He wasn't planning to be here long enough to witness the fallout.

Claire frowned. "Why? My sister, Jordan, and I were in foster care for a while after the first couple who intended to adopt us changed their mind. Foster kids aren't delinquents, they just aren't able to live at home for some reason."

"That may be true, but it's not people's perception. Red Hill Springs is a friendly little town, but people are set in their ways."

She stared at him, unflinching. Then grinned again. "Then I'll just have to change their mind." She leaned over the plate and took another big bite of pancakes as she slid out of the booth. "Gotta run. I have to make sure the fence line will keep my horse in."

Claire walked up to the register, where she chatted with his mom for a few minutes. She stopped back by the table to say, "Don't forget to bring Amelia out this afternoon. We can talk about rent then, if you like the cabin."

His eyebrows drew together. "I still don't get it. You don't even know me. And I definitely don't know you."

"Maybe I have a soft spot for a daughter who never knew her dad." She tossed the words over her shoulder as she swung the front door open. "Plus, you're armed and I don't have a donkey yet."

Bertie slid a to-go cup of coffee in front of him as the door swung shut behind Claire. "She's cute and she seems nice."

His eyes were on Claire as she walked toward her car. "Yeah, maybe."

"Hopefully, Amelia will eat with you tomorrow." His mom smiled as she reached for the dirty dishes on the table.

He laughed softly, shaking his head. "Who knows?"

"Well, don't give up, bud. She reminds me of someone else I knew once who was pretty bullheaded. Besides, you need her."

It wasn't until he was on the street walking back to his mom's house that he realized his mom had said *you* need *her.* That was ridiculous. Daughters needed a father, not the other way around.

But there was something there, some restlessness inside that he couldn't identify. His mom had said God was preparing him for something big. Something risky.

Like moving-across-the-country-to-start-a-foster-home risky?

He curled his fingers into a fist and stretched them out one by one, refusing to wince at the pain that shot up his arm. Sometimes just getting through every day seemed like a risk.

Chapter Three

Claire shoved the pole into the slot on the fence, tested the fit and fell against it, trying to catch her breath. She dusted the gloves on her pants and pulled them off, stretching her fingers. Her whole body ached. She hadn't expected to have to rebuild the whole corral when she arranged for Freckles to be trailered in today.

A honking horn caught her attention. She smiled, something easing in her chest as her twin sister, Jordan, pulled into the lane in her truck.

Jordan shoved the gear into Park and jumped down, enveloping her in a huge bear hug. "Wow! It's been too long."

"Hasn't even been a week yet."

Jordan's reddish-blond hair was twisted into two short braids and she was dressed, as usual, in boots, jeans and a flannel shirt. They were fraternal twins, but people had a hard time even believing they were sisters. She shrugged. "I'm not the only one who thinks so. Freckles went into a depression after you left."

Claire lifted the latch on the trailer gate, lowering it gently to the ground so as not to spook her horse inside. Freckles turned his head and sniffed, one big brown eye catching sight of her. He snorted.

She laughed as she climbed in and patted his rump. "I get it. You're mad at me now, buddy, but come January, when you're not trying to find the one remaining blade of grass under a half foot of ice and snow, you'll be thanking me."

He nudged her with his nose and she pulled out half an apple she'd scrounged from her car. After a good scratch and a minute to warm up to her again, she backed him out of the trailer. The second his hooves hit the ground, he lifted his head and sniffed the air.

"It smells different, doesn't it, boy?" She scratched along his mane and patted him before she turned to Jordan. "I don't know how to thank you for bringing him."

"No problem. How is it?"

"Rough. The whole place needs to be renovated."

Jordan walked a few steps away, taking

in the property. "What do you think he was doing, Claire, leaving us this property? He didn't know us, barely spent two hours with us once he found us. Was it guilt?"

A familiar hollowness settled in Claire's chest. "I don't know. Maybe. It's not like it's a giant prize. It's a mess."

Jordan walked a few steps, her hands on her hips, then turned back with her arms out-stretched. "Yeah, but it's awesome. Just imag-ine the organic vegetable garden over there to the left, the pond stocked with fish. A load of teenagers doing all the chores and cheerfully learning to be responsible."

Claire snorted a laugh as she walked her horse in a large circle. "You do have rose-col-ored glasses. When did you ever know teen-agers to be cheerful about chores?"

"Hey, there's always a chance." Jordan's blue-green eyes were shining.

"I'll call you and let you know how that goes."

Jordan leaned on the fence to the corral, fac-ing Claire. "Yeah, about that."

Claire stopped midstride. Behind her, Freck-les went still, glanced at her and went to nib-bling the green grass around the fence posts. "What?"

"I want to move here and work with you."

"In a second! But you know I can't afford to pay you." She led Freckles through the gate to the corral, where, for the time being, there was still some grass. She unhooked his lead rope and looked, really looked, at her sister. There were lines in Jordan's face that hadn't been there last week and she looked tired. "What aren't you telling me?"

"I lost the lease for the barn and the land. I have sixty days to get the horses moved somewhere else. I was thinking maybe you would be interested in having hippotherapy here. It would be great for your foster kids."

Claire's heart sank. There was nothing that would make her happier than having Jordan as a partner and being able to provide that kind of service for the kids, but she couldn't afford it. "Jordan, I'm not sure I have enough money to get this place up and running, much less for the upkeep of twenty horses."

Jordan leaned over the fence to scratch Freckles between the ears. "I thought about it all the way here. I have some money left from the life insurance, which I'll throw in, but it still won't be enough. I'll sell all but four horses and start over. There's nothing keeping me in North Carolina now that Mom is gone. Honestly, I don't know why I didn't think of it before."

Claire studied Jordan's face. Her sister loved a joke, but it was clear she wasn't kidding. "We'll have to work on the barn."

Jordan grabbed her and pulled her in for a tight hug. "We will. It's going to be amazing."

"Do you want to stay the night? This place isn't ready for overnights, but we can find a hotel somewhere close."

"I really can't. This timeline is a killer. I need to get back on the road while there's still daylight." Jordan's face lit up. "Oh, I almost forgot. I brought you a present."

She walked to the trailer and opened the door of the first compartment and reached in for a lead line. A very pregnant goat came barreling out.

Claire laughed. "Mama Goat?"

Jordan looked to the sky and shrugged. "What can I say? She missed you, too." She pressed the rope into Claire's hand and squeezed it. "Man, I wish I could just stay right now. I would love to help with the reno."

"I know. I promise there will be plenty of work left when you get here." Claire rubbed between Mama's horns, the familiar scratchy head so welcome after the day she'd had yesterday. She looked up at Jordan and clamped her lips together so she wouldn't beg her sister not to leave. She took a deep breath. "Sixty days?"

"Sixty days." Her twin and forever best friend hugged her tight enough to cut off her breath, ran to the cab of her truck and swung into it. As she drove away, she yelled, "Send me pictures!"

Claire laughed. Thoughts whirled in her mind, so fast she couldn't even grasp them. It was a dream come true to have Jordan with her, but Jordan's decision slapped another layer of responsibility onto an already teetering pile. She had to get this place up and running, and now, with four more horses coming, getting the barn ready would have to be a priority.

Plus, she was going to have to get Mama Goat a friend or she would eat everything in sight.

Her never-ending list just got a little bit longer, but there was only one way to handle it: one thing at a time. And lots of chocolate.

Joe turned into the drive at Red Hill Farm. Before he'd even come to a stop, Amelia was out of the truck and running toward Claire, long dark hair flying. "Hey, Claire, is that your horse? Is that a *goat*? What's her name?"

"Yep, that's Freckles, my horse. And this is a very pregnant goat who doesn't really have a name other than Mama Goat." Claire met his eyes, a smile lighting her face from within.

Her jeans and boots weren't fancy, nor was the ponytail, and she was covered in dirt. But despite her near breakdown the first day, it was obvious she was comfortable in her skin, comfortable in her abilities. Determined to make things work.

She handed the lead rein to his daughter. "Why don't you think of one for her?"

Amelia's eyes widened, then she looked away, playing it off. Joe hid a smile. "Yeah, okay, cool."

"She might need a walk. She had a long ride to get here."

Joe leaned over to scratch Mama Goat behind the ears. She butted him with her head and Amelia laughed, a delighted little-girl laugh, and Joe had to blink back tears. He hadn't heard so much as a giggle since she'd moved in with him two weeks ago.

Claire leaned back on the fence and her horse nibbled at her hair. She either ignored him or didn't notice, her eyes on Amelia. "When I went in the barn this morning to shovel out a stall for Freckles, I found a mama kitty with four little babies."

His daughter bounced on her feet. "Can I see them?"

"Of course. The mama's a little wild, but the kittens are small enough that they could probably be tamed." Claire appeared to think about it. "They'll need a lot of attention and petting. I'm not sure I'm going to have time with all the renovations."

Amelia's eyes widened, but she shrugged. "I could help." She shot a sideways glance at Joe. "Maybe."

Joe's heart clenched as he watched his daughter battle with hope. There'd been so little of it in her life.

"Are you sure? I could use a hand with the animals, but you're busy with school and stuff."

"I don't mind! I really don't." Mama Goat found something edible in the grass and put on the brakes. Amelia tugged on the lead, her forehead furrowing.

"If your dad says it's okay, it would be awesome if you could help me for an hour or two in the afternoons when you're free. But only if your dad says it's okay."

Amelia lifted her head, her big blue eyes meeting his. Those eyes that so mirrored his were full of uncertainty. She'd spent the last two weeks of her life trying to make his miserable and now her dearest wish was in his hands. "Please, Joe?"

He'd tried everything to figure out a way to connect with his daughter and Claire had just served it up to him on a silver platter. "Yeah, I think it's a great idea."

"Thanks, Joe! Claire, is it okay if I see if I can find them? I can put Tinkerbell here into the barn." It wasn't any of the grateful scenarios he'd imagined—Amelia didn't smile or hug him—but she had spoken to him of her own free will.

One step at a time.

"Tinkerbell is the perfect name. I love it! While you look for the kittens, your dad and I are going to check out the cabin on the other side of the pond." Claire started around the water's edge. The sun was easing toward the horizon, the sky streaky with pink and orange fingers of light.

Joe followed Claire, for once glad that the sunglasses he wore hid his eyes. Amelia had such a hard time trusting, but Claire had seen that the animals were a key to reaching her and hadn't hesitated. Maybe it was just his daughter, but Claire definitely had a way with kids.

The small cabin was tucked into the woods behind the main house. The place had obviously seen better days, but even in the current condition, the view of a crystal-clear spring-fed pond went into the pro column. A rocking chair or a swing on this porch would be really nice.

She pushed open the door and let him walk in first. He took off his sunglasses and tucked them in his front shirt pocket. Dust swirled in the dim room. It had a kind of charm, if you went for dark and brooding.

"It was apparently a foreman's cottage in the years Red Hill Farm was a working plantation. I thought it might make a good office for me, but it's going to be a while before I get to it."

He didn't say anything. She was obviously optimistic. It might make a good office, if she plowed it over and started again. Did he really want his daughter here? He opened a cabinet door and it fell off its hinges.

Claire jumped as it hit the floor. "Wow. Maybe this wasn't such a great idea. It's going to take a lot of work to make this place livable."

He heard a suspicious rustling sound in the bottom cabinet and elected to ignore it. "Let's just check it out."

"What's going on?" Amelia bounced into the space, her eyes sparkling even in the dim light, a tiny black-and-white kitten cupped in her hands.

"We're looking to see if the cabin might work out for us."

Hope burst onto Amelia's face and she danced into the front room. "We're going to *live* here?"

Joe sent Claire a look over his daughter's head. "Not necessarily. And only for a while, until my shoulder is better."

"Please, Joe. I'll help with the chores. I'll do whatever you ask." Her eyes brightened as inspiration struck. "I'll eat breakfast every day."

A small smile escaped Claire's control, but she didn't say anything.

Joe tried to summon his mean cop face, but the hope that this might be some kind of breakthrough with his daughter kept it from being very effective. "You'll eat breakfast with me? Without an attitude?"

Claire shoved one of the front windows up to let some air into the musty space. "Don't answer that, Amelia. You should probably check out the bedrooms before you decide."

Amelia looked around. "It's not that bad. We could paint it."

"There are two bedrooms with a bathroom in between." Claire sneezed.

"There's a bathroom?" Joe raised an eyebrow.

"No need to go outside. Amenities are assured here at Red Hill Farm. The place is really small, though, smaller than I thought at first glance last night."

"It's not small. It's cozy." Amelia ran from one room to the next, then popped back out into the main room. "Here, hold the cat. Can I have the bedroom on the right?"

"Uhm, sure." It was pure reflex that had Joe cupping his hands around the little kitten. It looked as stunned as he felt, little black eyes blinking at him. Amelia had gone from not speaking a word to chattering away, and it was weird. *Twilight Zone* weird.

Claire lifted the baby from his hands and snuggled it under her chin. "Tell you what, why don't we forego the rent for now? You fix the place up in your spare time. Clean it up, coat of paint, buff the floors. And when Amelia's not working in here, she can help me with the animals."

The *Twilight Zone* thing was still kind of buzzing in Joe's head, but he had the good sense to nod. "Yeah, fine with me."

Amelia bounced on the bed in the room she'd picked, a cloud of dust pluming around her. Claire shook her head. "I'm pretty sure I'm getting the better end of that deal."

Joe coughed, made a face, then coughed again. "You're right about that. We'll come back tomorrow after school and get started cleaning this place out. Amelia, it's time to go."

They stepped out into the light and Joe slid his sunglasses on. "Why don't you come back to Bertie's with us tonight? She'll have some kind of huge dinner and expect me to eat it all. Plus, if you're not there, she's just going to be grilling me about you. If you come, you'll be doing me a favor."

Amelia butted in. "Come to dinner, Claire. Stay in the guest room. I heard Gram say she wanted you to."

Claire hesitated but finally nodded her head. "If I can keep Amelia to help me get the animals fed and settled, I can meet you there for dinner."

"Done. I'll see y'all there shortly." Joe strode toward the barn and his truck, turning back for a second to look at the ramshackle place he'd just agreed to live in. It was either the best decision he'd ever made or the worst, but either way, they would be moving back to Florida when his arm and hand were fully rehabbed. He'd prayed for something to break the ice with Amelia, and at least they'd be working on it together.

First thing on his list was a mousetrap. Or a cat. He called back to Claire. "Hey, how long is it gonna take that cat to grow up and catch mice?"

She laughed. "Sorry, my friend. Longer than you've got. Maybe Mama Kitty will help you out."

Joe shook his head, stomping the mud off

his feet. He slid into the driver's seat of his truck. "Bye, Amelia. See you at dinner."

His daughter lifted her head from nuzzling the kitten and waved. Would wonders never cease?

He wasn't naive enough to believe this was the end of the reign of silence with his daughter, but he was so thankful for the reprieve.

After dinner with Joe's family, Claire sat on the front porch, rocking the swing gently with her foot. She was sure there was something she should be doing, but right now it felt so good just to stop. Stop moving, stop thinking, stop planning. Just breathe.

There were a few random sounds, a trash can lid clanking, a bell on a kid's bicycle, but mostly it was just peaceful. The back door creaked open. Joe stepped onto the porch and held out his hand. Four chocolates sparkled in their multicolored wrappers. "Ah, you do know the secrets of womankind, Joe Sheehan."

"Two sisters." He sat down in the swing beside her, his body weight setting it off kilter. "No secrets, just being observant like a good cop would."

Claire looked into those mesmerizing blue eyes. "You know you're taking on quite a challenge with that cottage. All joking aside, I'm not sure the thing would hold up against a strong wind."

He took a swig of his coffee and leaned back, stretching his arm the length of the seat back. "I know. But then there's Amelia."

Claire laughed softly. "You don't have to explain. I get it. My sister is moving here next month with four of her own horses so that we can do therapy with the kids. I can't afford five horses. But my sister needs me. Then there's someone else's kid who just might be unlocked by time on horseback. And you see how this goes."

"I do, actually. A month ago, maybe not, but now...I'm starting to."

"The idea is to give them structure through a schedule, belonging through their contribution, unconditional love from the animals and the people. It doesn't always work. But sometimes it does."

"Having unconditional love worked for me." His voice deepened, roughened with emotion. "If Frank and Bertie hadn't taken me in, no telling where I would've ended up. My mother...well, my mother was like Amelia's, maybe worse."

She glanced at him with sympathy. "Which makes it even harder for you to forgive yourself because you know what Amelia's had to deal with. Do you know where your mother is now?"

"No."

The answer was short. She got the point. He didn't want to talk about his mother. "Do your sisters and brother live in Red Hill Springs?"

"Ash does. He's the local pediatrician. You might've seen his office on Main Street. My sister Jules owns the bakery next door to the Hilltop. She lives just outside of town."

"Wait. So, your brother's name is Ashley and your sister's name is Jules?"

"Yep, Juliet. And my other sister's name is Edwynna. She goes by Wynn. Mom was all about leveling the playing field, giving all the kids gender-neutral names so that, for example, if they were putting a résumé in somewhere, no one would know if it were a man or a woman. Her name is Alberta, but she's always gone by Bertie."

"So you were the only one with an identifiably masculine name."

"That's true, but since my brother, Ashley, insisted on calling me Josephine, it didn't help that much."

A laugh burst out as his words sank in. "And where's Wynn now?"

"Wynn graduated from law school, passed the Bar and has been working for Congressman Schofield in Washington, DC, for the last two years."

"She sounds like a classic underachiever."

Joe laughed again. "You got that right. I don't think she's been home in three years."

The lump that formed in her throat surprised her. "If I had a home to go to, especially this one, I'm not sure I'd be able to stay away." He glanced at her sharply, and quickly she covered. "I mean, the food alone would bring me back. Your mom's a genius."

She and Jordan had each other, but since Mom died, they didn't have a family. No place they belonged simply because they existed. That was part of what she hoped to create here. Roots. She wanted to sink them deep into the rich soil of Red Hill Farm—for the kids who came through here, yes, but also for herself. She needed them.

Joe eased back in the swing, his hard jawline softening as he spoke. "I've gained weight just in the few weeks I've been back here. Food is Bertie's way of saying she cares about you. When I first came to live here as a kid, she left a plate of cookies by my bed every night. Maybe I should try that with Amelia."

Claire filed that away in her mind: nothing said love like a plate of warm cookies. A big black Lab ran under the streetlight and into an adjoining yard as its owner slammed open a door and yelled its name. It seemed such a friendly thing to do.

So many fears threatened to swamp her—the move, the finances, the decisions. There were moments, though, small little snapshots when she knew she'd done the right thing. She needed to hang on to these glimpses for later when her sanity would be questioned and her resolve tested. Because she had no doubt that it would be.

She turned her head quickly back to Joe. His finger jammed in her eye. She gasped.

"Oh man, I'm sorry. It was just a...I mean it was..." He stumbled over his words and she started to laugh, her hand glued over her throbbing eye.

"Are you okay?" His voice was miserable.

"No worries. I'm sure I can rock the pirate look." She peered up at him with the one good eye, sympathetic tears for the other eye flowing out of it. The look on his face was priceless. "Aargh, matey."

He grinned. "You had a...just a..." His hand hovered awkwardly around her face, and then he gently tucked a flyaway piece of hair behind her ear.

No more joking. She went still, her eyes flying open, both of them, to look into Joe's icy-blue eyes, which seemed kind of warm right now, to be honest.

He cleared his throat. "You know, now that you've been to the diner and the word is out, you'll probably have visitors all day tomorrow."

"Why?"

"Well, they want to size you up. See if you look like the old mayor, report back to their friends. And they'll bring you stuff."

In her mind, she imagined a rocking chair, a puppy, a sack of unshucked corn and other absurd things arriving on her porch. "Like what?"

"Some will bring baked goods—cookies and pies. Some maybe something they canned last summer. Their favorite family recipe they take when people are sick. Those are always good. My favorite is the funeral potatoes. Mmm-mm."

"You're terrible." She laughed. "They're good, though?"

"Oh yeah."

"Well, I better get an early start if I'm going to have to be stopping to visit and eat every few minutes." She stood and stretched. "What a nice evening. Thank you for making me feel welcome."

He stood and opened the door for her. "You *are* welcome."

"Thanks, Joe." He'd stepped up behind her, and when she turned back to thank him, she was staring at his chest. Dragging her eyes past his muscular shoulders, she met his eyes and forced herself to hold them. *Not interested*, she reminded herself. "I'll see you tomorrow."

"Probably pretty early. I have PT in the morning, and then I thought I'd get to work on the cabin. Maybe snag some of the funeral potatoes when Mrs. Jewel brings them over."

She laughed and started through the door. "Feel free."

"It's good that you're here, Claire. This town needs someone like you."

"If by that you mean headstrong and a little nutty, then I've definitely come to the right place. I'll see you in the morning." He was just being nice, she thought as she walked through the living room and down the hall to Wynn's room. Just being kind to someone new in town.

Not even having the energy to undress, she grabbed the throw from the end of the bed and pulled it up over her as she sank into the down comforter.

Obviously, she was exhausted. Otherwise, she would never be entertaining thoughts of how attractive Joe Sheehan was. A good night's sleep was all she needed to get these crazy thoughts out of her head. That and a little hard labor on the farm tomorrow should take care of it. Because even momentary feelings for the handsome cop could completely derail her plans and their friendship.

Chapter Four

Joe pulled his old Ford truck to a stop by Claire's back door. He checked the readout on his phone. No messages. He should be grateful just to be alive, and he was, but the lack of action unsettled him. In Florida, he'd been on a busy, well-funded, multicounty crisis response team.

In Red Hill Springs, he wasn't a peacekeeper. He wasn't a great dad. He tried to work out, but if he was honest with himself, while he was making progress, he wasn't strong enough on his right side yet to push it.

When he thought about it too much, the fear crept in. Fear that his injury wouldn't heal enough for him to reach the standards of the crisis response team. But deeper, the fear that without the CRT, there wasn't anything to him.

He wasn't a cop. He wasn't a soldier. He wasn't anyone's hero.

And yeah, he realized a shrink would have a field day digging into why he felt like he needed to be a hero to be okay.

He stepped out of the truck just in time to see Claire toss another avocado-green cabinet door on the pile by the back steps. She smiled at him as she brushed her hands together. Dust flew up from her work gloves and she laughed.

Tucking the bags under his elbow, he walked toward her, feeling conspicuously clean, although he had a premonition that wouldn't last long. "Hey, looks like you've gotten a lot accomplished. How long have you been at it?"

She rubbed sweaty curls away from her face with her forearm and then made a face as she realized it was as dirty as her gloves. "Fed the animals at dawn and then started in the kitchen in between making calls to various contractors."

A saw buzzed, voices raised over them. "Power company?"

"Yes, and an electrician on the inside of the house to hopefully fix anything that might come up with the wiring. The crew leader didn't seem very hopeful that it would be back on today, but still. Where there was only a tiny ember of hope, there's a small flame now. So we're on the right track. Maybe."

He followed her into the kitchen, where she'd already removed most of the cabinet doors. The table was covered with a tarp and crammed full of jellies, jams and baked goods from what had to have been a near constant stream of visitors.

Joe grinned. He'd definitely called that one. "I came to do a little work, but in the spirit of neighborliness, I brought you something, too."

He dangled a pale pink paper bag from his fingertips.

She narrowed her eyes. "You didn't bake something?"

"Nah. I figured you'd need real food by now."

Joe watched as she pulled out an overstuffed chicken salad sandwich on his sister's home-made bread. She shot him a look and took a huge bite, mumbling as her eyes closed in bliss.

"Mmm, that is so good. If I had coffee, I would be…" Her voice trailed off as he reached into the other bag and pulled out a paper to-go cup. "Wow. You might be my favorite person. Did you get this here?"

"Yep. At the bakery in town. My sister Jules's place." He dropped a larger brown paper bag onto a stray chair. "Not as good as

Jules's chicken salad, but what's in this bag is also for you. New locks."

"That's so nice." She finished the sandwich and rubbed the crumbs off her mouth with the back of her hand, leaving a smudge of dust behind. He laughed but didn't bother telling her. He had a feeling she wouldn't care. It seemed to him that whatever this woman did, she took in huge gulps, inhaling every bit and breathing out joy, even though he knew she had to be worried about the future here.

He wanted to step closer, let some of that joy seep into him. God knew he needed it. Instead, he turned toward the door. "The locks were my mom's idea. She's very worried about you. You have a Phillips-head screwdriver?"

She reached behind her back, pulled the one she'd been using out of her back pocket and handed it to him. "I have a drill, but it's not charged yet. Tough without electricity."

"That's true. This'll do fine." He popped the deadbolt out of the back door and rekeyed it, the whole thing accomplished in about four minutes.

"Nice. Are you looking for work as a handyman?"

He looked up, the smile fading a bit. "No, I'm afraid my skills with a lock come from my checkered past. After Dad caught me stealing tools from his garage, he made me change the locks on every person's house that I ever burgled. Even though, for the most part, I only went in unlocked doors."

"I didn't know you had a felonious past." Claire picked up the tools and followed him to the side door.

"Mercifully, it was short-lived and mainly driven by hunger. Frank and Bertie took me in. They started feeding me and, somehow along the way, managed to give me a sense of right and wrong."

"Frank is your dad? Bertie's husband?"

"Yes, he passed away not that long ago. It was sudden." He gathered up the stuff and walked through the house to the front door and began the same process.

"And after he died, you came home?" She took the bolt and held it as he rekeyed the back door lock.

He screwed the brass plate into place on the edge of the door. "No, it wasn't quite that simple. Let's go do the ones in the ballroom, and then you should be good to go."

"So you got shot..." She was being curious, nosy really, but for whatever reason, he didn't mind.

"I got shot. I knew I would be off the team for a good six months at least and figured Mom could use the company." He worked the screws into place.

"Did you ever think about applying for the job of chief after your dad died and staying on permanently?"

He looked up at her, surprised. "No, that's funny. Pretty sure most of the town is still convinced that I'm a bad influence because I was a delinquent as a child."

"You were a child." Her voice rose, full of indignation on his behalf.

"Yes. Well." He sat back on his heels. "This thing with Amelia showing up out of the blue…I would never regret knowing her, but it definitely has reinforced people's ideas about my character."

"From what I hear, everyone thinks you're doing a great job with her. My source is Lanna at the Hilltop, but I'm pretty sure she knows everything about everyone in town."

He chuckled, picked up his tools and tested the lock. "She does. Okay, all done. Later we'll come back to these French doors and add a more defensive lock, but these'll do for now."

She started toward the door at the same time he stood and slammed right into him. His arms closed around her. His heart ka-blamming in his chest, he looked into her eyes. Mistake.

His breath caught. Her eyes were wide and

innocent and pure blue like the sky. And he wanted more. More closeness. More connection. More Claire.

She stepped carefully back, forcing a laugh. "Wow. I'm off my game today."

Joe took the thoughts of her that had invaded his mind and mentally shoved them away. Snagging the sunglasses he always wore out of his shirt pocket, he slid them on as they walked into the kitchen. He laughed and, even to him, it sounded forced. "You have game?"

She responded with a delighted laugh and he nudged her shoulder and carefully changed the subject. "Just kidding. So now that you have the cabinet doors off, what's next?"

"I'm going with mostly open cabinets on the top, closed on the bottom. I'd love marble countertops in this kitchen, but that's not in the budget, so I'm going to put stainless steel on the island that's not built yet and concrete on the rest." She looked around, already seeing the finished product in her mind. "I want a huge island with a half dozen chairs—those metal ones painted all different colors—so the kids can sit there and do their homework or help with cooking. And a comfy couch and some chairs down there at the end by the fire."

"That sounds great." And it did. He could picture it in his mind. She was creating a home.

"I got a recommendation for a painter from the hardware store. He and his wife are coming to get started on the kitchen tomorrow, so I need to finish the demo today. You?"

A car pulled into the driveway. Through the hazy window, Joe saw Amelia bound out before his mom even got the car stopped good. "Joe?"

He grinned. "Headed to the cabin. I got some mousetraps at the store when I got your new locks. Maybe shouldn't mention that to Amelia, though. I'm afraid we'd end up with them as pets." He swung open the back door and stepped into the sunshine. "Over here, Amelia. See ya later, Claire."

Claire watched as he walked around the pond to the cabin she'd "rented" to him, his daughter bouncing happily beside him, and reminded herself. He was her tenant. A cop who had his own set of problems to deal with and she definitely didn't need more problems.

He wasn't even that attractive.

Yeah, whatever. Keep telling yourself that, honey. She eyed the plate of brownies that Mrs. Evelyn had brought. She wanted one, but she'd already had one and brownies were a treat, not a staple.

And that was how she needed to think of Joe. A sweet treat. Chocolate-covered? Definitely. But not the kind of thing she needed to make a part of her everyday diet.

A buzzing sound split the quiet and the lights flickered on. Her own whoop was nearly drowned out by the cheer from the guys working on her lines.

Things were looking up. She laughed and gave a thumbs-up to the guys working outside. She opened the door and hollered to them, "Make sure to stop by the kitchen and get some brownies and cookies before you go."

Another car turned into her lane and pulled to a stop behind Joe's truck. She sighed. At this rate she was never going to get the kitchen demo'd for the painters tomorrow and she couldn't afford to pay them to do the prep for her.

She walked out to meet her visitor, surprised to see a squad car in her driveway.

The driver, a man around sixty, stepped onto her driveway and hitched up his pants.

"Hi, there. I'm Claire Conley."

"I'm Acting Police Chief Roy Willis. I wanted to personally welcome you to Red Hill Springs." He looked around as he talked, his eyes lighting on the pile of discarded cabinet doors by the back steps. "You're going to need a construction Dumpster for that debris."

She was slightly taken aback but gave him

an easy grin. Rules were rules. She wasn't necessarily a stickler for them, but she got it. "I've got one coming, but I didn't have time to wait for it. I have painters starting work in the morning."

"Licensed and insured?"

"I'm not sure about that." Heat was starting to creep up her neck. She didn't know what the point of his questions was, but it wasn't against the law to hire unlicensed painters. "I hired them on the recommendation of the local hardware store, but I'll be sure to ask them when they arrive. It's a big project. They will have incentive to do a decent job because if they do, they'll have all the work they want for a while."

He glanced at the power company workers who were packing up, then back at her, a speculative look on his face. Surely he wouldn't have something to say about her having the power turned on.

"I have the proper permits to do the renovation on this property, Chief Willis. I had the attorney who handled the inheritance for my sister and me make sure of that."

He smiled, and instead of being reassuring, it increased her prickly feeling of unease. Whatever his motivations were in dropping by, she wouldn't be able to do anything if she didn't know. "Is there something in particular I can help you with?"

"Some people in town got the impression by the way you were asking around that you might be hiring day laborers. They were rightly concerned that you might be encouraging a...certain element...to hang around our town."

Claire wasn't even sure what to say about that. Some people in town were worried about it? People like him, for example? Her fingers clenched into a fist and she really just wanted to punch him in the face.

She wouldn't, of course. She had enough sense to know he was baiting her. He might be using his power to harass her—and that was exactly what she would call it—but she wouldn't give him the pleasure of hauling her in for assaulting the police chief, acting or not.

He leaned back on his car and crossed his legs, glancing at the cabin, where Joe and Amelia were going to be living. "We're a real friendly town, Ms. Conley, but it's my job to make sure that our town stays safe from riff-raff."

She really hoped that the electrician working in her house was not overhearing this conversation. For his sake and the sake of the other workers, she tried to keep her voice down. "I don't think that giving hard-working people a job is contributing to the 'riffraff' in this town."

"You would think, wouldn't you?" He smiled again, a smug, indulgent smile that said *bless your heart.* "Well, Ms. Conley, we have standards around here and we take those standards pretty seriously."

He looked again toward the cabin, where Amelia and Joe had disappeared through the front door. And suddenly she was smacked with the truth. This judgmental jerk wasn't talking about riffraff in general, he was talking about Joe!

Claire took a deep breath. Joe, Amelia and Bertie had welcomed her to town before she'd barely crossed into the city limits. There was no way she was letting this guy get away with spreading malicious lies. If he thought she would, he better think again. She didn't care if he was the police chief, he was going to have to get off her property.

"No, no, get under it, Amelia, it's gonna fall!"

Amelia squealed as her feet slipped out from under her on the dusty floor and the aging mattress landed on top of her.

Joe ran around the bed, jerked it off and dropped to his knees beside her. Her skinny arms were over her face and he could see her shaking. He reached out to touch her and pulled his hand back. A few days ago she wasn't even talking to him. He wasn't sure she would welcome his touch.

The fickle fall Alabama weather had turned cool again and she was wearing denim shorts and a sweatshirt with some furry boots that all the kids were wearing this year. She was covered in dirt. And he had no idea what to do with her. Call 911? "Amelia? You okay? Is there anything I can do?"

She threw her arms away from her face and he saw her big smile, small white teeth in an even row. The laugh spilled out as she grabbed the hand he held out to her as he tried to hide his sigh of relief that she was okay.

"Trying to get rid of me already?" She brushed the dust off her shirt, long dark hair sliding forward to cover her face.

It was a joke, but one that sent pain spearing through him. She'd been allowed to think he didn't care for far too long. He said quietly, "I don't want to get rid of you."

She glanced up at him, stared into his ugly, scarred face and patted his cheek. "Thanks. I don't want to get rid of you, either."

He wasn't sure if she believed him, but

he was going to keep saying it until she did. "Wanna go again?"

"Yeah, but I want to keep the bed part and paint it, okay? So don't break it."

"I'm not gonna—" Her dark eyes were twinkling. She was joking again. He was going to have to get used to this side of her. "Okay, okay. First we have to get the mattress out of here. So grab your side again, but this time get your weight under it."

He could totally haul the mattress out on his own, but she needed ownership in this house, this life they were building. And he needed to know they were in this together. "Ready...one, two, three, go."

She lifted her side, staggered under the weight a little and followed him out the door. From the steps, they tossed it onto a growing pile of trash. Amelia let out a cheer and held up her hand for a high five.

He obliged and said a silent prayer of thanks that finally—*finally*—he was breaking through the barriers to knowing his daughter.

She frowned. "Who's that yelling at Claire?"

Joe followed her gaze to the plantation house. Amelia was right. Claire was standing beside a police car. She had both hands out to the side, and while he couldn't see what she was saying, her mouth was moving fast. "Stay here."

Amelia shot him a look. "No way. I'm not letting that guy give Claire a hard time."

He didn't stop to argue with her. It was probably pointless anyway. He started toward the house. The man standing beside the car looked like Roy Willis. If it was Roy, purposely giving her trouble, Joe was going to have to do something about it. Things were not exactly rosy between him and the guy who'd once arrested Joe and chafed, big-time, with the fact that Joe had been adopted by the chief of police. He'd had the nerve to use Joe's adoption against Frank in an attempt to get him fired. It was small-time politics and Joe hated it.

Roy's voice carried. He was saying something about "undocumented workers" and "harboring criminals." Claire, to her credit, didn't react. She only pointed out that she would be paying all the workers and that she would be sure to get their names and addresses so that she could issue a 1099 at tax time.

Joe couldn't hear what Roy said next, but as he got closer, he could see that the acting police chief's eyes were narrowed in on Claire. And whatever he said really made her angry.

She pointed at his chest and her words were crystal clear. "If you think any of the people on my property are dangerous and a nuisance, then you're really going to love it when I have a house full of juvenile delinquents."

Roy's eyes nearly bugged out of his head, but he didn't answer, just jumped into the car, threw the gear shift into Reverse and sped out of the driveway.

Claire watched him as he drove away and then turned on her heel and stalked into the kitchen, slamming the door behind her.

Joe's footsteps stalled as he tried to figure out what he should do next. Amelia stopped beside him and they contemplated the closed back door, her stance unconsciously echoing his.

"Maybe you should talk to her." Amelia looked a little unsettled. And even though Joe had seen Claire's emotional reaction to the house the first day she'd arrived, it hadn't been anything like what they'd just witnessed.

He glanced down at Amelia. "She's really upset. Maybe I should just give her some time."

"That's dumb. You're her only friend. You can't bail on her." She turned her back on him and started toward the barn. "I'm going to see the kittens."

His gaze followed his daughter as she stomped across the yard in those clunky boots. She disappeared from his sight into the shadowy barn. When he turned back to the house, nothing had changed. The door was still closed and Claire was still inside.

Amelia's words rang in his head. *You're her only friend.*

Nice to be put in your place by a twelve-year-old. Reluctantly, he started for the house, climbed the steps and knocked on the back door.

Chapter Five

Claire leaned over the sink and splashed cold water on her burning-hot face. Tears stung in her eyes, her humiliation only worse because Joe and Amelia had witnessed it. And to be clear, she wasn't mad at herself for putting Roy in his place. However, she had lost her temper, and for that, she was very sorry.

A knock sounded at the door. She took a deep breath and turned the water off at the sink. Maybe he would go away if she didn't answer the door. Maybe, but that would make her even more of a coward. She swung the door open and he stood there, an apologetic look on his face.

Joe cleared his throat. "Can I come in for a glass of water? I'm still not sure the pipes are working at the cabin."

He was so handsome and so sweet and something eased in her chest that he would even care. Wordlessly, she pushed the door wider open to accommodate his frame.

Grabbing a plastic cup from a bag on the counter, he filled it with tap water and stared into it for a minute. "It's probably not about you. This thing with Roy—he's not a fan of change."

Her breath was a rush of expelled air and he turned back to her.

She ran a hand through her hair and more of it tumbled out of the band she'd had holding it back. Frustrated, she jerked the band out and shook her hair free. "He said to me, 'You're stupid if you think people can change. Trash stays trash.'"

The brutal words were like a slap, even though she'd heard them just moments ago. Joe didn't speak for a minute, then pulled out a chair from the kitchen table and sat in it. "He's angry. And maybe he's not happy with what's going on here in general, but that comment, that was directed at me. He arrested me back when I was in middle school. I asked for a glass of water from the waitress at the Hilltop, and when she wasn't looking, I took a Danish from the platter on the counter."

Her mouth dropped open. He had to be kidding. "He arrested you for that? What were you, nine or ten?"

He nodded and she shook her head. "What a jerk. You were hungry."

"He said he had to teach me a lesson." Joe shrugged, the expression on his face carefully blank. "It didn't stop me from stealing. Nothing did, until Frank and Bertie took me in. It was their love and support—and food—that made the difference."

"I can't believe him."

"He doesn't like me. I really do think he believes that people can't change." He tilted the water cup and looked in it again as if some secret to human behavior would be found there. She wished it was that easy. "He doesn't think about the experience that I have as a cop, or on the regional crisis response team, or even in the military. All he sees is that kid who used to steal."

She closed her eyes, her words flooding her mind, her face going hot again. "I shouldn't have said that about a house full of juvenile delinquents. They're not. I was just so angry."

When she opened her eyes again, he was looking at her with understanding. "I'll talk to him. And maybe he won't do anything."

"You think?"

"You never know." His words were hopeful, but his face told a different story.

She grabbed a napkin from the table and held it over her eyes, slumping back in a chair. "My mouth always gets me into trouble."

"Claire, Amelia and I can stay with my mom instead of moving into the cabin. There's no reason to bring this thing with Roy to your door."

She whipped the napkin off her face. "Don't you dare let that bully keep you from doing the right thing for your family. Amelia loves it here and we're going to make sure she gets to stay."

"Speaking of, our future veterinarian went to check on the kittens. Maybe we should check on her." He stood up and tossed his now empty cup into the trash can.

"Baby animals do cheer me up." She grinned and held out her hand. He grabbed it, hauling her to her feet. "Thanks, Joe."

As she followed him out the back door to the barn, she realized that her passion for kids and for justice was what made her happy and fulfilled. It was what made her...her. But it was also her biggest weakness.

A weakness that Roy wouldn't hesitate to capitalize on.

* * *

Amelia bounced in the vinyl seat next to Claire a few days later. "I'm starving. I want blueberry pancakes."

"Me, too." Claire grinned and shot Amelia a look out of the corner of her eye. "When I ate yours the other day, they were the best pancakes I've ever tasted in my life. Just the perfect ratio of blueberries to batter. I don't know how any other pancakes could ever compare to those. They were perfect."

"You're kinda mean, Claire." Joe sipped his coffee.

She sighed. "Yeah, and that satisfied feeling will be even better chased with a short stack."

Amelia rolled her eyes but grinned, taking the ribbing in stride. The difference in her face and actions, even in just a few days, was amazing.

Lanna stopped by their table with her tray and coffeepot. "Hey, folks, what's for breakfast?"

"I'd like blueberry pancakes, please." Amelia spoke up first and Lanna's eyes widened.

"Okay, blueberry pancakes coming up." The waitress nodded at Joe. "What'll it be, Joe?"

"The same for me except with a side of bacon."

Claire looked up from the menu. "Me, too."

Lanna took the menus and tucked them under her arm. "Refill?"

Claire smiled up at her. "Not yet, thanks, though."

As Lanna walked away, Claire caught sight of a poster on the bulletin board beside the door to the kitchen. She couldn't see it all, but it said something about a town council meeting. She slid out of the booth, and as she got closer, the words came into focus: *Emergency Town Meeting. Help defend Red Hill Springs from juvenile delinquents and criminals. 7 p.m. Library Community Room.*

Defend Red Hill Springs from what? This had to be the doing of Roy Willis. He'd said she would be sorry. She guessed this was his way of firing the first shot.

If so, it was a pretty good one. Years ago, she'd learned to quiet the voices in her head, the ones that said, *You're not good enough. You don't have what it takes. Why do you even try?* Those old insecurities were only a murmur in her adult life, replaced with a hard-won belief that she was a child of God and worthy of love for that reason alone.

She rubbed the scars in the crook of her elbow, the lines where she had cut into her skin with a razor blade as a young teenager. The voice of insecurity had been really loud then. Roy's actions brought those old feelings of desperation and shame welling to the surface.

Bertie walked up behind her and put her hand on Claire's back. "Your food's ready, honey. I'll be there tonight, but not for Roy. I thought about tearing that sign down, but I think we need to handle this now."

"You think people don't want me here?" Her voice was small and she hated it.

"No," Bertie frowned. "But people are talking. Roy has them all stirred up. Come on now, eat your breakfast. You gotta have fuel if you're gonna take down a bully like Roy Willis."

"I'm not going to let him win, Bertie."

"I know, sweetie."

As Claire got back to the table, Joe took one look at her face and put his fork down. "What's going on?"

People in the other booths were starting to stare and she didn't want to make a scene. She lowered her voice and said, "Roy's apparently gotten the town council to hold an emergency meeting tonight. He's telling people we're a threat to the town's safety."

Joe's jaw set in a hard line. Amelia's eyes darted back and forth between the two of them. "What does that mean? What's going on?"

"Just a bully throwing his weight around."

Claire heard the words she said to Amelia, words that echoed Bertie's. Roy *was* a bully. And he was trying to intimidate her to make himself look better.

Joe picked up his fork to take a bite and ended up pushing his pancakes to the side. "I take full responsibility for this. I'll deal with Roy."

"This is not your fault, Joe."

"Hard not to take it that way when someone is using you to get to me." He leaned back in the booth and picked up his coffee cup.

"He's so consumed by himself that he doesn't realize he's not hurting you or me." Slowly, the fear she felt was becoming anger. She shook her head and took a vicious bite out of a piece of bacon. "He's hurting children because of his own agenda. And that's the worst part. It's important to fight for what's right, even when it's hard."

"I know sometimes the right thing isn't the most popular thing to do," Amelia said around a mouthful of blueberry pancake. She used the back of her sleeve to wipe syrup off her chin.

"Exactly." Joe handed her a napkin. "You can't give in to someone who wants to do the wrong thing just because you want to get along. Remember that when someone wants you to drink or smoke pot."

His daughter rolled her eyes. "Don't worry, Joe. I'd like to actually have a life one day."

A bell rang in the distance. Amelia sighed and shoved one last bite of pancake into her mouth. "Gotta go."

Claire let her out of the bench seat and then slid back in across from Joe. "She's smart. With some time and consistency, I really think she's going to be fine."

"I hope so."

Lanna refilled Joe's cup. "She's a good kid, Chief. She just needs a dad, and she has a good one."

Joe laughed. "I'm glad y'all are confident in my parenting skills."

Claire took one more sip of coffee and dug some money out of her pocket, placing it on the table. "I've got to go, too. The painters are supposed to be back at my place by nine."

"I'll be out there to work on the cabin and Mom will bring Amelia by to feed Freckles and Tinkerbell after school."

"Joe, you need to think seriously about whether you want to align yourself with me on this. Your family is here."

He dumped some sugar in his cup and stirred. "No, I don't. I knew there would be some eyebrows raised about turning Red Hill

Farm into a foster home. That doesn't mean it isn't the right thing to do."

She smiled, but inside she worried about how this would affect the reputation that he was trying so hard to rebuild. Maybe it was that old insecurity telling her she didn't deserve an ally and friend. "I'll see you later, then."

As she walked away, her smile faded. It was one thing to be willing to fight for what was right.

It was another to actually survive the battle.

Joe rolled the soft blue paint that Amelia had picked out for the living room onto the wall. The sting in his shoulder reminded him that he'd been shot a few months ago. That he missed his job. Missed his team.

It hadn't escaped his notice that he was building a home and a life here while he was longing to be back in his old life.

A splash and a scream echoed off the main house. He ran toward the spring-fed pond as Claire surfaced, spluttering and laughing. He had to grin as she did a backstroke across the pond. "So it's a little chilly?"

She lifted her head and smiled at him. "Yeah, slightly!"

"You decided to swim in your clothes?"

"No." She laughed. "I was on my way down here to bring you a Gatorade and I thought, it may be October, but it's really hot, I should take a swim."

"Sounds like good reasoning to me."

"Come on in."

There were about a million reasons he shouldn't. But her eyes were shining. And that was the one reason he should. Maybe jumping into the water without a care for how cold or how weird or even whether it might look foolish was the way to joy. And he'd already established that he needed more joy.

He stood there another minute, watching the water slide off her dark hair into the clear blue pond.

"It's amazing," she said, treading water. "Come on."

He kicked off his running shoes and started for the edge.

"Don't go slow. If you think about it too much, you'll chicken out."

He put one foot in the water and gave her his best *you've got to be kidding me* look.

Laughing, she splashed him. "Man up. It's just a little cold water."

Joe took a deep breath and dived in, surfacing beside her, gasping when shock took his breath away. For a split second, he was in an alley on the waterfront, staring at the sky, trying to suck in oxygen and failing. Deliberately, with slow deep breaths, he focused on the present. The bright blue October sky. The warmth from the Indian summer sun. He wasn't dying. He was very much alive.

"You okay?" Her perceptive gaze seemed to see right through any walls he put up.

"Yeah, fine." He lay back and let the cool water soothe his ragged edges, the ones where he wondered if this in-between time would ever end.

"Sometimes when there's so much going on, I have to stop and take a minute to remember why I'm doing…what I'm doing." Her voice broke through his thoughts and the quiet lapping of the pond.

"I got shot." The words strangled out.

"I know." Claire straightened and he knew she was looking at him, but he couldn't look her in the eyes.

"I've been injured before. I know how to come back from it. I'm just tired."

She didn't say anything and he closed his eyes. He shouldn't have said anything. She had so much on her mind and didn't deserve—

"I'm not sure this will make you feel better, but it's absolutely normal, what you are feeling. It's normal to feel anxiety, about being shot and about the future, to wonder if you'll ever get your mojo back, so to speak."

Her quiet words washed over him like the lapping waters of the pond.

"It's normal to feel isolated. It's normal to feel depressed. Normal to feel vulnerable. And it's very normal for those feelings to freak you out if you're not used to feeling them."

His eyes searched her face. There was no hint of judgment. "Thanks."

"You've had a lot to deal with. Any of the things that have happened to you would leave you reeling. Give yourself some time."

"I keep hearing that." Maybe at some point it would sink in. And he desperately wanted to change the subject. "Are you worried about the meeting?"

"Yes. I think I came down here hoping you would distract me. I have so much to do and what I keep doing is stewing."

"Don't give up. I don't know if you're that good with all kids or if it was just a special connection with Amelia, but if it wasn't for you, we'd still be deadlocked in the silent treatment with a plate of blueberry pancakes between us."

She smiled, but her eyes were shiny with unshed tears. "I'm not giving up. But thank you. I needed the reminder of why it's so important."

"I have the feeling that you're too stubborn to give up anyway." The tense moment was gone, thank goodness. He knew the trauma of being shot would surface again, but for now he'd gotten through it.

She laughed again and splashed the cold water in his face. "Oh, you do know how to sweet-talk me, Joe Sheehan. Let's do this again. Same time tomorrow?"

"If you promise to resuscitate me when my heart stops from the cold." He started swishing through the water toward the bank.

"That's what friends are for." She clambered out of the pond behind him.

As he watched her walk back to the house dripping a trail of water behind, the thought crossed his mind that he really liked her and he hadn't felt that way in a long time. The doors to his heart, so to speak, had been firmly closed. His past—his job—kept him at arm's length from other people. Seemed now there was just a crack in the door, enough to think...maybe.

But no matter how wide the crack was, there was too much—way too much—uncertainty in both their lives to add to it right now.

Claire turned and waved from the back stairs before disappearing into the house. He chuckled to himself.

She just had a way.

He sighed and got to his feet. Amelia would be here soon to feed the animals and then they were all going to the town meeting. Roy Willis wasn't one to back down from a stance he believed in, no matter how wrong it might be. Joe had a feeling Claire was in for the fight of her life.

Chapter Six

Claire's hands were clasped together tight enough to crush a pecan. Anxiety had been building all day until she was about to jump out of her skin. Or throw up. Or worse.

The only relief she'd gotten was the icy cold swim, which was just shocking enough to break her train of thoughts. At least for a little while.

She'd prayed all day, willing that the words she would say tonight would be God's words, not hers. If this project was just a figment of her own dreams, she didn't want it. It wasn't worth the price. But if opening a home for foster children was God's will, she knew Red Hill Farm and the children who would live there could make a difference in the life of this whole town.

She could feel the eyes boring into the back

of her head. People coming in had left a wide berth around her. Two seats on all sides. No one in this crowded little room wanted to sit next to the person who was going to ruin their town, but they all wanted to get a good look at her. She took a deep breath, straightened her shoulders and waited for Mayor Campbell, who was also the local banker, to stop working the room.

Finally, he walked to the podium in the library's community room and cleared his throat. The monitor squealed and he had to move the mic and podium a couple of times until it stopped.

Mayor Campbell cleared his throat again. "Welcome, everyone. As you know, we called this emergency town meeting to discuss some things that are very troubling. I know we all have families to get home to, or dinner warming in the oven, so I'm going to get right to the point and invite Roy Willis up to the podium to share some concerns he has. Roy?"

As Roy stood up and hiked his pants, Bertie slid into the seat beside Claire. "What'd I miss? Where's Joe?"

"Nothing yet." Claire took another deep breath and willed herself to relax a little. "He said he would be here."

Roy buttoned his coat and smoothed it.

"Good evening, everyone. I want to take this opportunity to thank you so much for coming out. I know how busy everyone is."

He had this gentlemanly air about him, which was the furthest thing from what she had seen at her house yesterday. He continued, "You all know I've protected and served this town for forty years. I have the town's best interest at heart. And when I heard about this woman's plan to bring delinquents and criminals into our town, I knew I needed to act."

Claire shifted in her chair. He was uninformed and acting like he was an expert. Bertie reached over and gripped her hand, tight.

Roy hadn't looked at her yet. In fact, he was avoiding her eyes. "Our community is a safe, friendly, God-fearing town. We're not afraid to let our children ride their bikes. We talk to our neighbors over the fence. Sometimes we might even forget to lock our doors. Do we really want to change our way of life because an outsider is planning to open some kind of halfway house for juvenile delinquents?"

Claire had known that juvenile delinquent statement would come back to bite her. She just hoped that people wouldn't fall for the false narrative that Roy was weaving for them.

Roy's gaze slid from face after face. "We have to applaud Ms. Conley for her desire to help people who are less fortunate, of course, but there's a reason we don't live in the big city. And, in my opinion, the big cities can keep their drugs and gangs, thank you very much."

There was some scattered applause at that. Claire's stomach churned.

"If you're as concerned as I am about our community, please join me in banning this kind of halfway house from our town."

There was more clapping, but not as much as there would've been if Bertie hadn't sent a quelling look around the room. The mayor stood and walked back to the podium. "Would someone like to make a motion that we vote?"

Bertie jammed her elbow into Claire's ribs, catapulting her to her feet.

The mayor waited for her to make the motion, clearly not realizing that she was the person at the center of this discussion. "Mr. Mayor, I'm Claire Conley. I'd like to say a few words, if I may."

He looked hesitant, but she took advantage of the pause and walked to the podium, where he gave her the floor. She cleared her throat and tucked her hair behind her ears, suddenly feeling very conspicuous in her cotton skirt and flats.

"My sister and I inherited Red Hill Farm from our biological father. When I met him shortly before he died, he told me what a lovely town he lived in and about many of you and what you meant to him. At the time, I was working with foster children in Charlotte, North Carolina."

Claire looked toward the back of the room and realized Joe stood there, his sunglasses in place, his arm around Amelia's shoulders. When she paused, he smiled and nodded encouragement to her. She relaxed her shoulders and returned the smile, meeting the eyes of people around the room. These folks were not her enemy, they were worried about their families, and she could understand that.

She focused on giving them something personal to think about, rather than some threat out there that no one could put their finger on. "After I found out my biological father left the house to us, I realized my sister, Jordan, and I could do what we'd always dreamed of doing—give kids a place to live where they would be safe and loved and could learn about a better life. I couldn't think of a more perfect place than Red Hill Springs for kids to learn about community and family and responsibility."

Roy stood, tucking his shirt in again. "'Scuse me, Mr. Mayor, but regardless of Ms. Conley's dreams, it's pretty much black-and-white. Do we want delinquents in our town or do we not?"

"I'd like to try to address Acting Police Chief Willis's concerns." Claire had to work at maintaining a level, calm tone. She smiled at Roy. "I appreciate your point of view, sir, but in this case, the facts don't support it. It's true that I'm renovating Red Hill Farm to house foster children, but most of them are very far from being delinquents."

Roy opened his mouth to retort, but someone spoke up from the back and he sank back into his chair. A young woman with a messy bun and a food stain on her shoulder was on her feet. "You said 'most' won't be delinquents. Does that mean you'll have some?"

Claire nodded. "That's a good question. Children who are in the foster care system come from difficult circumstances or they wouldn't be in foster care. It's not hard to imagine that some of them, not all of them, have stolen, or gotten in fights, or been kicked out of school. We'll address the root cause of those behaviors and give them positive things to focus on instead."

The mayor looked thoughtful. "What kind of things?"

"The plan is to have an organic garden, a fish pond, and domestic animals like chickens and goats that the kids will help take care of. It's possible, in time, that some of that produce will be available to the community." She paused. "Also, we'll start with five horses. The kids will take care of those, too, but they will also be used for equine-assisted therapy."

A guy in a ball cap stood up in the back. "I'm all for rehabilitation, but those kids will be in our schools, mixing with our kids. I don't think our children should bear the brunt of someone else's personal problems."

As the crowd murmured, Joe stepped out of the shadows in the back corner of the room. "All due respect, George, your kids will be bearing the brunt of someone else's personal problems, regardless. Either our community helps kids recover from trauma, or we pay for it later on when they're adults."

He walked closer to the front of the room. "Many of you know that my mother struggled when I was a kid. If Bertie and Frank Sheehan hadn't taken me in, I don't know where I'd be right now. I sure wouldn't be a cop."

Roy muttered something under his breath to the guy sitting next to him and received a glare from Bertie.

"Folks, listen. If you don't think our community needs to be a place where we help kids who don't have any place to turn, then so be it. But don't let fear and misinformation guide your decision. Get to know Claire. Talk to her about her plans. Mr. Mayor, I move that we table this discussion for a couple of months."

A guy in the front row whom she didn't recognize said, "Second."

The mayor stood next to Claire. "All in favor?"

The majority of hands in the room rose.
"Opposed?"

Roy and a few others raised their hands.

"The motion carries. We'll meet back in two months at the regularly scheduled council meeting to have a vote. And, Ms. Conley, I'd like to set up a question-and-answer time after church one Sunday, so folks can be better informed before they vote."

She nodded, thoughts spinning in her head. She caught the expression on Roy Willis's face before he turned to a group of people waiting to talk to him. Roy was angry. White-faced angry.

A young woman, one who'd been sitting next to the food-on-her-shirt mom, hesitantly approached. "I'm Jamie. I just have a question, if you have time."

Claire shook her hand. "Yeah, sure. I hope I have the answer."

"I have a four-year-old little boy." She held

out her phone and showed Claire a picture of a towheaded little guy holding a rabbit, not looking at the camera. "He's just been diagnosed with autism. I take him over to Mobile for therapy as often as I can, but I was just wondering about the horses. He loves animals. Would the horse therapy be available to people in the community?"

"Yes, definitely! Especially for little guys who can come during the day when ours will mostly be in school. He's adorable."

"Yeah, he is." Jamie looked down at her feet. "I guess it's pretty expensive."

"Actually, my sister, Jordan, and I haven't talked about it specifically, but I think we would provide services on a sliding scale, based on your ability to pay."

"Really? Oh, thank you." She turned to wave at someone in the back who called her name. "I have to go, but thank you so much. Please come to church on Sunday."

"Thank you, I appreciate that so much. I'd love to."

Joe appeared at her side with a pretty blonde woman about their age. "Hey, Claire, this is Ellen. We sat next to each other in Algebra class. Actually, I'm pretty sure Ellen cheated off my paper."

"Stop! You know that's not true. I made way

better grades than you." She looked at Claire and rolled her eyes. "He told his mom that last week!"

"So, Ellen wondered if you might have some ideas or encouragement about her son."

Claire smiled at Ellen, who looked suddenly nervous. "I'm happy to help if I can."

"I just wondered if maybe riding horses might help my son's confidence." She looked around the room and lowered her voice. "There's this big kid in gym class that picks on Wyatt. And Wyatt's not weird or anything, he's just kind of small for his age."

"Riding horses and learning to have control over such a large animal does help a lot of kids with confidence."

"Did that kid hurt Wyatt?" Joe interjected.

Ellen looked miserable. "He came home with a black eye on Tuesday. Y'all have to know it's hard for me to ask for help."

"You could have him arrested for assault, but it might not help." Joe crossed his big muscular arms. His mean mug was impressive. The fact that he was angry on behalf of a bullied boy made Claire's heart melt just a little more.

"I talked to the principal and to the other parents in the class a few weeks ago and it just made things worse for Wyatt." Ellen's eyes filled with tears. "I'm a single mom. I've never faced anything like this before."

Claire put her hand on Ellen's arm. "Bring him out tomorrow. I usually take a break from the reconstruction around four o'clock anyway. I'll introduce him to Freckles. The other horses won't be here for a while, but Freckles is a real gentleman."

"Are you sure?" Ellen's hand, over her mouth, was shaking. "I can pay you for lessons."

"We can talk about that tomorrow." Claire met Joe's eyes and he nodded almost imperceptibly.

Ellen pulled the strap of her purse back onto her shoulder and looked toward the door. "My dad is waiting. I need to go. Oh, I can't thank you enough. I'll see you tomorrow, Claire. Thank you so much."

"Thanks. She was always kind to me. It means a lot that you would try to help." When Joe nudged her shoulder, Claire looked up into his eyes. Her breath caught in her throat. He was gorgeous, yes, but those clear blue eyes revealed a strong, generous spirit.

"It makes my blood boil to think a bully is beating up her son." And honestly, it made her feel a sense of solidarity with the kid, since she was here tonight only because Roy Willis was a bully throwing his weight around.

She wasn't going to give in without a fight, either.

From the newly washed and now sparkling clean window of the cabin, Joe watched Claire with Wyatt in the corral. He could almost see her patience as she led the middle schooler in a walk and then coached him into a trot.

Ellen stood at the rail, her face full of hope that her small-for-thirteen-year-old son would find some confidence. And that, Joe knew well, Wyatt would have to do for himself. No mom or mentor alone could instill it in him. But what they could do was give him a different lens to look at himself.

He tossed the dust-coated rag into the trash bin and started around the pond toward them. Maybe clarity was what Claire was giving him and Amelia, by giving them a different lens with which to see each other and themselves.

It was working, in some ways. Amelia was starting to not only think of herself as the victim of an absent father and he was starting to forgive himself for not knowing she existed. They both had a long way to go, but they were making progress.

Ellen smiled a greeting as Joe walked up, but her chin trembled. "He's doing great, isn't he?"

Joe nodded. "Yeah, he is."

"He needs to learn some other skills, too."

"Like what?" He watched Claire coach Wyatt as he took Freckles on a slow solo spin around the corral.

"Well, his dad left when he was a toddler, and while he adores my dad, Pop-Pop just isn't going to teach him how to land a solid punch."

Joe laughed. "I'll be happy to hang out with him, but I'm not going to tell him to hit another kid. I could teach him some self-defense techniques, though." His eyes were on Claire, and though she didn't visibly react or look at him, a smile curved her lips.

"There you go, Wyatt. You show that big horse who's boss. And it's not him." When the boy used his heels to get Freckles away from a small, tasty patch of grass, she clapped. "That's the way! All right, take him over to the water trough and let's let him have a drink. You did great for your first lesson!"

Wyatt slid off the big gelding to the ground. He wasn't smiling, but he squared his shoulders and carefully gave Freckles's hindquarters a pat as he walked behind.

Claire released Freckles into the pasture and turned back to them, an easy smile on her face.

"Ellen, I'm ready for a cup of coffee and a snack. How about you?"

"Oh, I don't know..." Ellen looked worriedly at her son.

Sliding her arm through Ellen's, Claire half dragged her toward the house. "I have so much food from everyone bringing goodies. I need help."

Ellen's Southern manners kicked in and she looked helplessly at Joe as Claire led her across the backyard.

After watching them walk away, Wyatt squared his shoulders and turned to face Joe. He was skinny, his reddish-brown hair a silky mop on his head. Scattered freckles completed the picture.

"What are you doing with my mom?"

"Your mom and I are friends."

"Are you gonna kiss her?" At his side, Wyatt's hands curled into fists.

"What? No, I'm not going to— Dude, your mom and I were friends in high school. She sat next to me in Algebra. I copied off her page because she was smarter than me."

Wyatt's expression was shocked. "You're not supposed to cheat."

Joe smothered a laugh. He had to give it to the kid. Regardless of what his mom thought, he had some guts. "I know. I don't cheat now, but I didn't have a mom like yours to teach me stuff like that back then."

When Wyatt nodded at his mom's general awesomeness, Joe asked, "How'd you get that black eye?"

Immediately, Wyatt's mouth slammed into an obstinate line. Joe sighed. "Look, I told you about cheating off your mom in Algebra. I wasn't the brightest bulb, but I know about bullies. Want to tell me about it?"

"It started at the beginning of the year. These guys would make fun of some of us for being scrawny or, um, you know, not filling out our jockey shorts and stuff." Wyatt grabbed a water bottle from the top of a fence post and took a swig. "They didn't touch us or nothing until the other day. This one kid named Sheridan pushed this kid named Carlton, who has Down syndrome. He was just being mean, but it really ticked me off because Carlton started to cry."

"I can see why. I would've been mad, too."

"I told him to go away, but about the time I stood in front of Carlton, that kid Sheridan punched me in the face. I didn't cry or nothing, but I was kind of out of it for a while."

The desire to give that kid Sheridan what he deserved was almost overwhelming. Probably not the kindest feeling Joe had ever had.

"I know a couple things that might help you keep that from happening again. Want me to show you?"

"Uh, yeah." Wyatt followed Joe onto the grass. He showed Wyatt some defensive moves to keep the bigger kid from beating him up and a few things he could do offensively to get a bully to back down. Ellen's boy might be skinny, but he was wiry, and with a little help, it wouldn't be a completely one-sided fight the next time.

"So here's the last tip for today—speak with authority." He got in the kid's face. "Now, tell me to back off."

"Back off." Wyatt's voice cracked in the middle.

Joe tapped him in the diaphragm. "From here. Back. Off."

"Whoa, okay." Wyatt squared his shoulders and narrowed his eyes. "Back. Off. Sheridan." He sneered the last word.

Joe grinned. "Now, that sounds like you've got what it takes to back that up. Good job." A horn honked from the driveway, Wyatt's mom.

He made a face. "I've got youth group tonight. I guess I've gotta go."

With a fist bump, Joe told Wyatt he'd see him around.

As her son jumped in the car and buckled in, Ellen waved at him and mouthed, "Thank you."

He waved, and as Ellen pulled onto the highway, Claire appeared at his side with a cup of coffee. "Nice thing you did there, Sheehan."

"Yeah? Not so shabby yourself, Conley." He sipped the coffee and thought, surprisingly, that the crisis response team's highest adrenaline-producing moments couldn't compare to this one. Being with Wyatt and helping him gain some confidence and sharing the moment with Claire was the best.

He hadn't felt a moment like this in a long time. Questions milled in his mind, questions like was he really making the right choice to try to go back to his old job? The thought of leaving gave him a rocky feeling in the pit of his stomach.

He shook his head and pushed the thoughts deliberately away. Being a cop was who he was. He might be a dad and a son and a friend, but underneath it all, he was a cop.

Life in Red Hill Springs was appealing, more and more so, actually, but his real life was calling. And he was going back to it.

Chapter Seven

Claire waited outside the school for Amelia and, as she watched kids greeting their moms and dads, wondered if Amelia missed her mom. She thought about her own mom constantly, picked up the phone to call her at random times through the day before she remembered that her mother wasn't at the other end of a phone call anymore. Cancer had taken her so fast and left such a gaping hole in Claire's life.

Her mom would love that she was using her inheritance from her father to build something lasting, and something more than just wood and glass and appliances. Her mother believed in people. She would be proud that Claire did, too.

Amelia opened the door and climbed into the front passenger seat, dumping her backpack to the floor with a thud. "Hey."

"You got the message about me picking you up, I take it." Claire started the car and gingerly pulled out into the after-school traffic.

Joe's daughter clicked her seat belt into place. "Yeah, Joe's at his doctor's appointment. Where's Gram?"

"She had an emergency come up at the café. Something about a dishwasher or refrigerator or something. Either she or your dad will pick you up at the farm later on."

"Cool. Can I see the kittens?"

"Of course. I have snack food, too."

"I figured. Joe told Gram that your kitchen is like a convenience store."

Claire snorted a laugh. "Sounds about right. I'm painting the bedrooms, if you want to help."

"I'd rather play with the animals. Are you still sleeping in the dining room?"

"Yep. Until I get the bedrooms finished."

Amelia unzipped her backpack and dug around, coming out with a little ball with feathers attached to it. "I got this for the kittens."

"They're going to go crazy for it." As Claire turned into the long driveway at the farm, she rolled the windows down. It smelled like grass and dirt and fresh air here. A haze hung in the sky from the dust of crops being harvested. She loved it.

Amelia took off like a streak for the barn as soon as Claire stopped the car.

"Hey, girl, your backpack?" Figuring it was a lost cause, Claire picked it up and about fell over at the weight. She yelled toward the barn. "I'm going inside to paint for another hour or so. Check in with me every half hour, please."

Amelia stuck her head out the door, a kitten already tucked up under her chin. "Okay, I will."

"Cokes in the cooler, snacks in the kitchen. You know what to do." Joe's daughter was already gone. Claire laughed softly. "Another one bites the dust."

She and Jordan used to say that when her foster kids would go to the barn for therapy. It took about ten minutes with the horses for them to fall completely in love.

Animals were magic with wounded children.

An hour later, with the sun going down, Claire wrapped her brushes in plastic wrap and went looking for Amelia. She found her lying in the grass in the backyard with the kittens romping around her.

Grabbing a couple of snack cakes from the counter, she headed outside. She sat down in the grass and, as Amelia pushed up to one elbow, tossed her a Swiss cake roll. "What're you thinking about?"

"Nothing, really." Amelia unwrapped the snack and took a bite. "I guess just about how my mom dropped me off and didn't even check to make sure my dad was there."

Claire's heart felt like lead in her chest. She took a bite of her snack cake and chewed, weighing her words. "That had to be really scary."

Amelia dropped her head back to the grass and stared blankly at the sky. "I knew she didn't take good care of me, but she's my mom, you know?"

"I do." Claire lay back on the grass beside her, looking into the fluffy clouds, pink from the setting sun. "You know, it's okay to love her, no matter what."

A tear streaked from Amelia's eye into her hairline. She rubbed it away, sneaking a glance at Claire, who pretended not to see. "My dad's trying really hard. I was mad at him for a while, but it's not his fault my mom couldn't keep it together."

"I think your dad will do anything he can to keep you safe. And he wants to make you happy, too, but it's still okay to be sad about your mom."

Amelia rolled her head toward Claire.

"When I was eight, my mom said we were going to go watch the fireworks on the Fourth of July. Instead, she got high and had a seizure. I found her in the bathtub. I thought she was gonna die." She paused for a long minute. "My mom didn't go to rehab, did she?"

"I don't know, Amelia." Claire had answered questions like these more times than she wanted to think about from foster kids. It was always painful. "Do you miss her?"

"Yes. Kind of. But with my dad, I'm not worried about food or whether he's going to forget me at school." The sun was sinking and in the twilight Amelia looked older than her twelve years. "Do you think Jesus is looking out for my mom?"

Tears lodged in Claire's throat and burned her eyes. This time she was the one blinking the moisture away so Amelia wouldn't see it. "I know He is, honey. He was looking out for you when He brought you to your dad and He's looking out for your mom right now."

"We should get the kittens back in the barn and check on Tinkerbell before dinner. It's almost time for her baby to be born. I noticed she scratched all her hay into a pile today, just like you said she would." As quick as that, the moment was gone. Amelia bounded to her feet and pulled Claire to hers. "And after dinner, I'm gonna beat you at cards."

Claire laughed. "Not a chance, but I'll let you try."

As Amelia took the kittens back to the barn, Claire wondered if she'd said the right things. The questions were big questions. And some, like whether Amelia's mom would allow Jesus to help her, only time could answer.

She looked down the long drive out to the highway where Joe had left to go back to Florida, just for a visit this time, to check in with his doctor and the crisis response team he was a part of in Florida. She'd been praying for him all day, that things went well, and if they didn't, that he had the strength and faith to deal with it.

Joe pulled slowly into the driveway at Red Hill Farm. Claire had texted him hours ago to let him know that Amelia was with her and could stay the night, but he hadn't returned the text. He'd finished his appointments and driven out to the beach, planning to stay only until he found some peace. Usually, the ocean calmed him. Not today.

He got out of the truck and walked toward the back door, lifting his hand to knock. The back door opened and bright yellow light spilled out onto the porch. He lifted his head and found himself looking into Claire's worried blue eyes. "Hi."

She looked beautiful and perfect with a blue smudge on her face. He reached a finger out and brushed it down her cheek. "You've been painting."

Her eyes widened slightly at his touch and he realized for the first time that he wasn't the only one who felt a pull.

Deliberately, he let his hand drop and smiled, a slow, tired smile. "You still got my girl here?"

"She crashed about an hour ago, after she ate dinner and beat me to a pulp in Crazy 8's."

"Mind if I take a look at her?" He wanted to see her and remind himself that she was what really mattered, not him.

Claire led the way through the kitchen to the small family dining room that she'd converted into a makeshift bedroom. It was messy, a hodgepodge of clothes and tools and painting supplies. And it smelled like fresh green apples, like Claire. Not an ideal bedroom— Claire was obviously roughing it—but Amelia seemed entirely at ease, her arm thrown out in sleep. His daughter was safely tucked in bed and the knowledge that there were times when she hadn't been nearly killed him.

"She's been through a lot, but I think she's

going to be okay." Claire reached out to him, but he didn't grab hold. Not because he didn't want to, but because he was afraid he wouldn't want to let go. He felt adrift and Claire was strong and steady, her passion for what she was doing, solid and real. Instead, he walked through the kitchen and onto the back porch.

From the open door behind him, Claire said, "I have barbecue chips, plain chips, cheese curls and tortilla chips. A selection of candy and snack cakes as well, if you're hungry."

Joe winced. "She told you I said your kitchen is like a convenience store?"

"Mmm-hmm." She walked out the door and stood beside him, looking at the stars in the sky.

"Well, do you even have a piece of fruit in there?"

She scoffed. "Of course I have fruit. There are fruit gummies on the counter, a whole box of them."

"Fruit does not come in a box." He shook his head, but as he looked back at the glittery sky, he realized the knot of worry he'd been carrying in his chest had started to loosen. She had a way of doing that with animals and children, and, apparently, him.

"Wait till we have things growing in our garden. You won't be able to move in here for all the zucchini and tomatoes." She backed down the stairs as she was talking. "I need to peek in on Tinkerbell. Tell me about your appointment while we go check on her. If you want to."

He followed her across the yard, but talking about the doctor's report and his team's decision wasn't high on his list at the moment.

Claire pushed the door to the barn open. She wasn't even through the door all the way before she turned back, her voice an urgent whisper. "Go get Amelia! Tinkerbell's having her baby."

She disappeared through the door again.

Joe ran for the house and slammed open the back door. "Amelia!"

He bolted through the kitchen and into the dining room. "Amelia!"

She sat up in bed, rubbing sleep-drenched eyes. "Joe? What's going on?"

"Claire needs you in the barn."

"Tinkerbell?" Amelia was wearing a long lavender nightshirt that had to belong to Claire. She jumped to her feet, shoved them into the work boots she'd left by the back door and started down the steps before skidding to a halt and turning back.

"Joe, come on!" She dashed across the yard, nightshirt and hair flying behind her. By the time he picked his heart up off the floor and got to the barn, the hard part for Tinkerbell was over.

"Okay, Amelia, dry him off." Claire grabbed a suction bulb out of her kit and quickly suctioned the baby goat's nose and mouth.

Amelia crooned to the new baby while she rubbed it all over with a clean, dry towel. "Oh my goodness, you are so cute. Isn't she cute, Joe?"

It was mucky and sticky and kind of gross, to be honest, but also incredibly cool. His daughter didn't pay any attention to the mess. She concentrated on her job, and when they moved the baby for Tinkerbell to clean, Amelia sat back on her heels with a completely satisfied look on her face. "Twins!"

"What? Nice!" Joe peered around the door of the stall and realized that Tinkerbell had already delivered one baby, which was tucked into her side. As Claire placed the new baby by her head, she began patiently cleaning it, too. It was like she just knew what to do out of instinct or something.

He would give a lot to have that kind of innate instinct with Amelia. He leaned against the wooden post. "What are you going to name them?"

Claire's twinkling eyes met Amelia's. "Peter Pan and Wendy, of course."

He chuckled. "Of course. I don't know what I was thinking. So, what's next?"

"Amelia needs to go home to bed because she has stuff to do tomorrow. I'll stay out here with Tinkerbell for a while. There are a few more things to do before I can turn in."

"Can I spend the night? I want to see them in the morning. Please, Claire?"

"Only if it's okay with your dad. He's had a long day, too."

Truthfully, there were only a couple of hours before daylight. It wouldn't hurt to let her stay. "Go wash up. I'll be in soon to tuck you in."

As Amelia walked slowly into the house, Joe watched Claire. She took a small mason jar full of dark liquid out of her kit, along with shiny silver scissors and some white string. She glanced up at Joe. "There's an extra sleeping bag in the trunk of my car if you want to stretch out on a piece of floor near Amelia."

"I'm fine right now. What are you doing?"

"Checking the umbilical cord and dipping it in iodine so they won't get an infection. Want to help?"

He nodded, so she handed him the first little goat—brown-and-white Peter.

"Just turn him over and I'll do the rest."

Joe let the little goat lean back on his chest while Claire made quick work of tying off and dipping the cord, then switched and handed him Wendy. They were still kind of damp but starting to fluff up. Wendy blinked dark brown eyes at him. He held firm until she nuzzled him under the chin with her nose, and then he was a goner. He scratched under her tiny chin and whispered in her ear that she was going to love it here.

Claire encouraged each of the newborns to nurse from Tinkerbell, who obviously just wanted a nap. He could relate, but watching those fuzzy little goats so new in the world had somehow eased the pain from the day.

"I'm just going to shovel some fresh wood chips and straw in here for Tink and her babies, and then I'll be in, if you want to go check on Amelia."

He started to walk away but turned back to her. "Claire, thank you. I know you didn't plan this, but it helped, so thanks for letting me be a part."

"No problem, anytime." She didn't look up from what she was doing and didn't realize that his face probably reflected what he was feeling. That she rocked his world every bit as much as Amelia's, with her optimism and her warmth, her easy acceptance of him. And he was getting used to having her around.

Joe shook his head.

He needed to get himself together, because no matter how much he liked and admired Claire, his future was a murky blur. It wouldn't be fair to her to start something when he had no idea if he would even have a job at the end of his six-month leave.

Claire shoveled a fresh load of wood chips into Tinkerbell's stall. She could imagine how Joe felt, from firsthand experience. Horses and goats didn't talk much, but they were warm and real and somehow they had a way of helping you narrow things down to what was really important.

Tink was tired out from her ordeal and protested when Claire moved her onto the fresh straw. Both babies had full tummies and were ready to settle down, too. Maybe they would all get a nap this morning. She laughed out loud at that thought. The goats would, for sure, but a nap for her? Not likely with the day she had ahead.

A soft breeze blew toward her across the pasture as she walked out into the yard, and she had to admit that her inheritance looked like a graceful old lady in the predawn haze. She dragged her tired body to the picnic table behind the house and sat on top of it, taking in the last few stars twinkling in the sky, remembering the promise she'd made to her mom before she died, that she wouldn't waste a second.

Her mom was one of those people who when you met them, you didn't have a doubt that you had just met Jesus. Claire longed for that kind of relationship with Him. She wanted to breathe in Life and breathe it out in her every action. She wanted the kids coming to this home to know Him, too.

And she wanted to be brave, like her mom had been. To not be afraid to do hard things just because they were hard. She rubbed the old scars in the crook of her arm. Sometimes it wasn't easy to battle those feelings of inadequacy, of not being good enough.

The screen door shut behind her, and a few seconds later, Joe appeared at her side with two cups of steaming coffee. "Since you drank mine the other day at the Hilltop, I figured if I fixed yours the way I like it, you'd be okay with it."

She took the cup and smiled. "I would drink the cold dregs of a three-day-old pot right now and be grateful for it. This is so much better."

"You probably need sleep more than coffee." He sat on the table beside her, their feet together on the bench.

"I do, but in a few minutes Freckles will be standing by the fence waiting for his feed and the cat will be out here on the porch meowing for her breakfast. By the time I get them fed, the workers who promised to come on a Saturday will be here. But if all goes according to plan, by the time the sun goes down, the rotten boards on the front porch will be replaced and the downstairs paint will be finished."

Joe cupped the coffee between his two hands. "Your day makes mine look simple. I've got physical therapy this morning, but hopefully this afternoon I'll be at the cabin, painting, too."

"How'd your appointment go today?"

He shrugged, looking into his cup. "They're not sure I'll be able to get back to full strength. There was some nerve damage." He cleared his throat. "They offered my stand-in a permanent position."

"Oh, Joe, I'm sorry." She grabbed his hand, gripped it.

He looked down at their intertwined fingers and ran his thumb over hers. "It's…I kind of expected it, but I still have to try. You know? It's what I do, who I am. So I have a couple of months, give or take, to get back to a hundred percent or I'm done on the team."

"There's more to you than you give yourself credit for, I think." She paused. "Are you going to be okay?"

He blew out a breath, and when she glanced at him, he was staring across the pond to the cabin, where he and Amelia planned to live. "To be honest, I'm not sure. I've always had this reputation of calm under pressure. I mean, I got paid to handle stressful situations. To use my brain to figure out what makes people tick and talk them down. But all of this has me twisted up inside."

"I get feeling out of control. Believe me." The last few years had been an exercise in learning to trust that even if she didn't understand why things were happening, God did. Helplessness, grief, loss, fear. She knew about those, too. "Whatever I can do to help, I will."

"I know. And that means a lot." He bumped shoulders with her one last time and stood up. "Amelia fell asleep facedown on the mattress still with her mucky boots on. Are you sure you don't want me to take her back to Mom's and bring her out later?"

Claire stood up and stretched her tired back. "Nah. Let her stay. She can sleep in and help me around here when she wakes up."

His blue eyes narrowed. "Are you sure? I don't want to take advantage of you."

"Pish. Didn't you hear the part when I said I was going to put her to work? Besides, you know she would be pestering Bertie about getting back out here to see the babies. And you already said she could."

"Yeah, I did, didn't I? All right, then. I'll be done around noon. I'll bring food when I come back. Like some apples or broccoli or something."

"Ha-ha." She threw her wadded-up cup at him and pointed to his truck. "Leave."

He laughed—a real, genuine laugh—and a weird warm fuzzy feeling started in her stomach. *Off-limits. Off-limits. Off-limits*, she silently chanted to herself, but she smiled at him as he swung into the seat of his old truck.

She watched him drive down the long driveway and wave as he pulled out onto the highway. She picked up her crumpled cup and headed inside for a fresh cup of coffee, but her thoughts were still on Joe. He related to what she was doing here in a way that most people couldn't. He was sexy and sweet and, wow, really wounded.

And despite all the denial and lecturing herself about what was acceptable?

She was totally falling for him.

Chapter Eight

Joe hefted the last gallon of paint from the back of his truck. He'd hit the home improvement store after leaving the physical therapist and he and Amelia had been painting nonstop since midday. He glanced across the pond to Claire's house, where he could still hear the pounding of a hammer, Claire's porch being repaired.

"Come on, Joe. We're burning daylight." His daughter leaned on the column holding up the tin roof of the porch and he quickly prayed that it was strong enough to hold her up. So much of this cabin was held together on a spit and a prayer.

He swung the gallon of paint onto the porch. "Last one. This one is for the bathroom. It's neon green."

"Lime green." Amelia rolled her eyes and he

smothered a laugh, keeping it to himself that the green was so bright it hurt his eyes.

"Did you wash the hot pink off the brushes?" Joe had seen her at the hose with the brushes while he was getting the next gallon of paint.

Picking up a brush, she flicked water on him. "Oh, sorry. I guess it's still wet from me washing it."

He calmly walked to the hose and picked it up, pretending to wash his hands. Instead, he put his thumb over the spout and sprayed her.

Amelia shrieked, dancing as the cold water hit her. Ducking her head, she ran for the bucket where she'd been washing the brushes, picked it up and doused him with it, all the while squealing and laughing at the top of her lungs.

He dropped the hose and fell back on the ground, arms stretched out, belly-laughing. She splatted to the wet grass beside him.

"And here I thought I was going to be rescuing Amelia from a boring day of painting." Claire walked toward them with a large picnic basket. "But it looks like I interrupted a water war."

Amelia scrambled to her feet. "Joe just decided to spray me with the hose for no reason."

He cut his eyes toward her. "Uh, no, I distinctly remember you spraying me first with that paintbrush."

"Well, I figured y'all might be hungry, so I brought some sandwiches down." She walked over to the steps and sat on the top one, oblivious to the water streaming down. She dug into the basket and tossed the first sandwich to Joe. "BLT."

He studied the sandwich suspiciously. "You brought us sandwiches you made?"

"You're safe this time. I called the Hilltop and put our order in with Bertie."

He and Amelia had been so busy he hadn't even thought about eating, but he was starving. "In a week or so, we'll have a kitchen and you'll be knocking at our door."

"I'm a fan of pretty much anything I don't have to cook." Claire crumpled the tinfoil from her grilled cheese into a ball, tossed it into the picnic basket and took a bite. "So, you're probably right."

"What are you going to feed the kids who live with you?"

"I know how to cook. I'm just not fond of it." She considered. "Maybe I'll make Amelia my chef."

Amelia choked and then said, "Sorry, but I already have a job. You made me the assistant to the animals."

"Oh, right. I guess I'll have to come up with a different plan. Maybe one of the kids who is placed here will know how to cook."

"Maybe you can take lessons from Bertie."

She widened her eyes. "Or… Bertie will be my chef."

"Might be a little hard to convince her to leave the restaurant."

"There's that. Guess that puts us back to one of the kids cooking. Anyway, you're great at pointing the finger at me, but who does your cooking right now?" She tilted her head. "Methinks that might be the pot calling the kettle black, my friend."

"Methinks?" He grinned but conceded the point graciously. "Maybe Mom will teach Amelia how to cook. Boom. Perfect solution."

Joe hadn't noticed Amelia getting more and more quiet during their conversation until she shot to her feet, tears pooling in her eyes.

"Hey, what's wrong, kiddo?"

"You think you're so smart, making all kinds of plans for me. You don't even know if I'll be here in six months. You don't even know if I'll be here next week." She didn't stop to let him reply, just swung around and took off around the pond toward Claire's house.

He started to say something but ended up

just heaving a confused sigh. "I thought things were going so well today."

"They are. She probably never had an adult keep promises, but she likes it here, with you. She just doesn't know how to make plans. She probably never could before."

Joe knew what that felt like. He'd lived that very bleak life, just existing from one day to the next day, focusing on having something to fill your stomach or scraping up enough cash to pay the water bill. "I can't believe I didn't realize. Should I... Yeah, I should go talk to her."

"She's probably in the barn."

He was already on his feet. "Yeah."

Joe walked around the pond. He did understand what she was going through. Even as an adult, he still had a hard time trusting people. He should've seen this outburst coming. And maybe that was exactly what he should share with her.

He pushed the door to the barn open enough to slide into the shadowy, cool building. For a long few seconds, he couldn't see anything, but as his eyes adjusted, he found Amelia in the very back stall with the kittens. Mama Kitty was nearby giving him the evil eye, her tail twitching in annoyance. Giving her a wide berth, he slid down the wall to sit on the floor of the stall, draping his arms over his knees.

"You can leave." Amelia's voice was thick with tears and he had to resist the urge to pick her up like a small child and hold her. And he would if he thought she would allow it.

"I'm not going anywhere." He sat quietly for a moment, watching her. She was sitting cross-legged on the floor of the stall. The kittens were curious, climbing around her feet. "I want to tell you a little bit about what it was like when I was growing up, if that's okay."

She sighed and closed her eyes. "I already know you were adopted by Gram."

"Do you know how old I was when I was adopted?"

She opened her eyes but didn't say anything.

"Thirteen. I spent the first twelve years of my life moving from one condemned house to the next, dreading summer because I wouldn't have anything to eat without the free lunch at school. The only time I ever saw my mom was when she broke up with her latest boyfriend or if she ran out of money for smack and came home to kick me around a little bit."

Tears glittered in her eyes again. "I didn't know that."

"I know, it was bad and I don't talk about it that much. But, honey, that part really doesn't matter as much as what I'm about to say. What I want you to remember, really remember, is that I would never have left you in that kind of situation if I had known about you."

"I know." She sniffed back tears. "I love my mom and I miss her."

He nodded, but his chest felt like it had been sliced open. Not that she cared about her mom, because of course she did, but that she should have to be thinking about all this instead of just enjoying being a kid.

"I don't want to live with her anymore, though. Do you think that's okay?"

"I think it's one hundred percent understandable that you would feel that way. And I promise that I will do everything I can to make sure that you're the one who gets to make that decision." He looked at the kittens, who had given up and curled into a ball of little furry kitten ears and backs and tails. "I get why you like the animals so much. They give you love and don't expect anything in return except for love back."

She ran her finger down the back of the nearest kitten. "Yeah, I guess. I mean, Claire has to feed them."

He laughed, and his chest ached because he loved her so much. "Yeah, that's true. What I'm getting at is that I want you to try to think of me like you would one of the animals, at least for now. I love you and I'll be here for you. I don't expect anything in return. You get to be a kid for a while. Let me take care of the other stuff."

"You love me?" She scrubbed at one tear-streaked cheek.

He scooted closer to his daughter and put his arm around her. "From the first second I laid eyes on you."

She laid her head on his shoulder and, heart nearly exploding with the force of love he felt for her, he prayed. He was kind of rusty, but being a good dad wasn't something he could do on his own.

Please, God, help me do what's right for her and give me wisdom to make good decisions. Don't let her feel abandoned and unloved ever again. "It's gonna take time, honey, but we'll figure all this out. And I hope someday you'll know that you can trust me because it's worked out for you to do that, not just because I say so."

"Me, too." Her voice sounded so small. Sometimes she seemed so mature that he had to remind himself that she was just a child, but she was. A child who had been on her own a long time, but one who still deserved a childhood in a hot-pink bedroom.

He nudged her. "Hey, you know that neon-green bathroom isn't going to paint itself."

"It's *lime*." She grinned and he knew the crisis had passed, at least this crisis for this moment.

He scrambled to his feet and held his hand out for her this time. "Come on. We better hurry or Claire might be finishing it up already. That woman never sits still."

Amelia giggled as she pushed open the door of the barn. "She was painting the inside of the bathroom closet when I got up this morning."

"What did you have for breakfast?"

"Frozen pizza." She giggled again. "With orange juice."

"Sounds pretty good, actually." The sunlight speared through the trees and dappled the ground. He put his arm around his daughter as they walked and he just…knew. There was nothing he wouldn't do to protect her.

Sunday, church morning. Claire's hand hovered over the doorbell outside Bertie's house. She didn't want to bother Bertie with such a lame problem, but she'd put most of her things in storage so she could travel light and somehow managed to not have anything to wear to church. As in, not one item of clothing without paint or rips or stains. Even the skirt and shirt she'd worn to the council meeting now had a paint splotch right in the middle.

This was stupid. She couldn't knock on their door at seven in the morning. For all of Bertie's generosity in welcoming Claire to town, she was still a virtual stranger. She turned to walk away and the door flew open behind her. A voice, not Bertie's, said, "Aren't you going to come in?"

Claire turned slowly around, heat rushing her face. A gorgeous young woman stood in the door in a T-shirt and cotton shorts, holding a mug of coffee in her hand. Definitely not Bertie.

Way to make a first impression, Conley. "I was just leaving."

"You must be Claire. Mom was telling me about you last night. I'm Joe's sister Jules." She smiled and brushed long, flowing honey-blond curls over her shoulder, out of her way.

Bertie shouted from inside, "Let the girl come in off the porch, Juliet."

Jules blinked and smiled as if she were sharing a joke with Claire. "Mom's cooking breakfast. Cinnamon rolls. You really should stay."

"I'm not sure… I think I need to be going."

"Fix you a cup of coffee, Claire, and tell me why you're here." Bertie elbowed the door back, her hands covered in cinnamon, sugar and flour.

She took a deep breath. "I don't have anything to wear to church. All my stuff is packed away, so unless jeans and paint-splotched T-shirts are welcome at church, I'm out of luck."

Jules looked her up and down. "She's about Wynn's size, don't you think, Mom?"

"Yes." Bertie nodded as Jules started toward the hall. "Good thinking."

Jules grabbed her by the hand. "Come on, Claire. I haven't raided my sister's closet in years."

Claire followed Joe's sister into the bedroom Claire had slept in the night she'd stayed with Bertie. Jules threw open the closet and flipped through a few dresses. "Try this one. And this one. Oh, here, this one's cute."

Amelia came bursting through the door. "Hey, Claire, I didn't know you were coming over."

"Me, either. I had a panic attack when I realized mucky boots and jeans ripped at the knees weren't going to cut it at church today."

"They should." Jules matter-of-factly held up a dress to Claire. "This one. It matches your eyes. I'll look for a scarf and boots while you try it on."

"Thanks." Claire slipped into the adjoining bath and pulled off her sweats and T-shirt, sliding the soft blue dress over her head. She looked in the mirror. It nipped in at the waist, making her look small, and was just the tiniest bit swirly at the knees. She loved it.

Outside the door, Jules called out, "So what's the deal with the town council? Mom said they were having a conniption about foster kids in your home?"

She pushed the door open and Jules smiled. "Good, I was right. It fits perfectly. So, the foster kids?"

"There's some question about whether they will be delinquents and put the town at risk."

Jules rolled her eyes and draped a scarf around Claire's neck. "Our resident cop was quite the delinquent in his day and look how good he turned out."

"Joe?" Amelia was incredulous.

Joe himself appeared in the door. "I heard my name. What are you filling my daughter's head with, Aunt Jules?"

Jules shooed him back into the kitchen before pointing at the cowboy boots on the floor. "Try those, Claire. They look like they might be the right size. Fortunately, Amelia, your dad found Jesus, for which we were all profoundly grateful."

Claire glanced at Amelia, who was looking pensive after the revelation about her dad. "Everyone has a past, Amelia. Even parents."

She sat on the edge of the bed, now covered with dresses, and tugged one boot on, then the other. They pinched a little, but nothing she couldn't live with. "They're great. Thank you so much."

"No problem. That outfit looks nice on you." Jules kicked back on the bed and looked at Claire. "So, the town council."

"Right. I'm just trying to get to know as many people as possible in town and reassure them."

"You do have your work cut out for you. First, you're living in the former mayor's plantation home because you're his illegitimate daughter." Jules ticked it off on her fingers.

"Yes." Claire laughed. It sounded so ridiculous when Jules said it out loud.

"What's illegitimate?" Amelia bounced up to sit on the bed beside Jules.

"Never mind," they both said at the same time.

Jules held up a second finger. "Then you have the nerve to strike up a friendship with the town's reformed bad boy."

"I can see how that would be concerning to the town council." She winked at Amelia, who grinned.

"Then you have a crazy plan to use your inheritance to give a home to homeless children... Yes, I can definitely see how that would be a red flag." Jules rolled her eyes again and sent Amelia into gales of laughter.

Claire wiped tears from her eyes. "It sounds like you've got a handle on things."

"I should. I lived here all my life. You better believe there was some talk when Mom and Dad adopted Joe. They didn't let it stop them from doing the right thing."

Bertie stuck her head in the door. "The cinnamon rolls are ready. Come dig in before Joe eats the whole pan. And stop talking about your brother when he's not in here to defend himself, Jules."

Amelia giggled and followed her grandmother down the hall. Jules shook her head at Claire and shrugged. "She always did have supersonic ears. Never could figure it out. Ash spent a lot of hours looking for hidden microphones but never found any."

Claire slid to her feet and started toward the kitchen for one of Bertie's famous cinnamon rolls. Another thing to tuck away in the imaginary file named Bertie's lessons for parenting. Make your children believe you are magic.

Chapter Nine

Joe joined the crowd milling around outside the church. He pretended to be looking for his mother but had his eye out for one specific person. There was a lot more to this town than the town council meeting made it seem, but it was hard to see beyond the accusations from Roy and his cronies. He wanted to check on Claire.

He spotted her across the lawn and started toward her, nearly mowing down his brother, Ashley, in the process. "Dude. Watch where you're going."

"I was, Josephine. You're the one who plowed into me." Ash followed Joe's line of sight to Claire. "Ahh, the new star of Red Hill Springs gossip. She's cute."

"She's nice. Amelia likes her."

"Amelia likes her, huh? How's the little squirt doing? Filling out any?" His brother grinned, his famous dimples making an appearance. Joe would swear that every woman in a ten-foot radius turned to look. Ash, with his model-blond hair and those darn dimples, was like a woman magnet. It was annoying.

"Looking better, finally. Mom puts food in front of Amelia every time she slows down." Amelia had been severely underweight when her mother dropped her off. She'd gone hungry. A lot. A knot formed in the pit of Joe's stomach thinking about it.

"Good. If you want me to check on her, bring her in one day this week. Now, I'm going to talk to the woman who will single-handedly give me a bump in my practice when all the delinquents come to live with her."

"They're not delinquents, they're just kids."

Ash grinned and tossed the words over his shoulder. "I know. It's just so much fun to annoy you."

With a sigh, Joe followed his brother through the after-church crowd. A hand on his arm stopped him.

"Here's the man who helped me get the cows back in the pasture yesterday. He didn't even curse when his foot got stepped on. He has some kind of way with cows." Mr. Haney chuckled. He gripped Joe's sleeve as he talked, the group of old men surrounding him widening as the story spread.

"It's some kind of way, all right, Mr. Haney, but I'm not sure what. Obviously, I didn't do much. I think I might need to borrow your cane for a while until the bones in my foot heal, though." The group of men laughed, one of them slapping Joe on the back, another looking at him with grudging respect.

This group didn't have to be told that Mr. Haney needed help. As his neighbors, they'd been helping him out with his livestock constantly since his stroke almost a year ago. In this community, that was just what people did.

In fact, it wasn't like this community at all to back someone into a corner the way they did Claire. With him, it was a little easier to understand. The memories people had of Joe were of him being a juvenile thief and, even after he was adopted by the Sheehans, a bit of a troublemaker.

But the residents of this town cared about each other and they cared about the children who lived here. Surely it wasn't too much to expect for them to reach out to children in need.

Extricating himself from the group he'd been chatting with, he searched the yard once again for Claire. He found her leaning against a low brick fence, smiling as she talked to the small group of people around her. She was wearing a pretty blue dress that matched her eyes. Her hair lifted slightly in the whisper of a breeze. And his brother, Ash, was standing next to her with his arm draped around her shoulders.

The urge to punch Ash in the face didn't surprise Joe. He'd had that feeling often enough. It was the reason he wanted to punch him that surprised him. He really didn't want his handsome doctor brother anywhere near Claire.

"If you'd like to come over for coffee," she was saying to the person across from her, "and see the house as it's being repaired, I'd be happy for you to come. Anytime." She smiled again and it was then that he realized things weren't what they seemed. Her smile was frozen and something was very, very wrong.

At that moment, Claire didn't remember Joe's brother's name. She only knew that his arm behind her back was holding her up. She was exhausted and overwhelmed. Somehow in the months leading up to her move here, she had neglected to imagine that there were people out there who genuinely cared more about themselves than they did about children who desperately needed a safe place to grow up.

The older woman sniffed. "This town was here long before you were and we're not going to let a newcomer with a do-gooder complex ruin it for the rest of us." She shook her head. "That beautiful old house…"

Claire's breath backed up in her chest, her ears buzzing.

Joe stepped into the circle. "What's going on? Mrs. Willis, is there a problem?"

Claire stretched her smile a little wider and shrugged slightly. "No problem. I was just leaving. Like I said, Mrs. Willis, my sister and I would love for you to visit anytime. I'm sorry to leave in a rush, but I have to get back to check on the animals."

She walked away, hot tears stinging her eyes, trying not to let anyone see how badly she was shaking. She heard voices calling after her. Joe, and probably his sister, too. Lanna, she thought, waved to her, but she couldn't really see through the haze of tears. Blindly, she walked to her car and got in and started it up.

Claire drove down the oak-shaded highway. It wasn't like she'd stolen her inheritance. The thought made her laugh. Why would she want to steal a broken-down old plantation house and spend tens of thousands of dollars renovating it?

Claire pulled into her usual parking spot beside the house and jammed the gear shift into Park, scrubbing the remains of the tears from her face.

She didn't need them. She didn't need anyone.

It took her about ten seconds to shed the dressier clothes that Jules had let her borrow and pull on jeans and her own broken-in boots. She grabbed her pale pink ball cap from the hook by the back door and strode to the stable. She hadn't been riding because she was too busy, but she and Freckles both needed a run.

She pushed her way into the dark, cool barn, whistling for him as she went into the corral. She didn't need a saddle or reins. Freckles knew her well enough to be guided by the pressure of her hands.

It took just enough concentration to stay seated on Freckles that all the negative thoughts could be pushed to the back of her mind. Her hair whipped behind her, and when she turned the corner and started back to the house, her hat flew off. She laughed out loud, letting the wind carry her laughter along with her hat.

What had she been thinking? She had no ties here. Only a dead father she never knew. A falling-down house. And a dream.

She laughed louder.

She had a dream. She leaned over Freckles's neck and whispered in his ear and he went faster.

The wind in her face, the sound of the hooves, her body moving in unison with her horse. Freedom whispered, *Leave it all behind.*

Freedom was going to have to stuff it. She wasn't leaving. She had a dream and a plan and she was going to make it happen. She let her feelings of inadequacy and not being enough fly away with the wind.

Freckles's pace dropped to a slow trot as they got closer to the house. She eased him into a turn, and as they neared the gate, she slid off his back to the ground. Nudging him toward the water trough, she patted him on the rump as she walked behind him into the corral.

Joe was leaning forward, his muscular arms crossed on the fence, long denim-clad legs and the boots... It was the boots that got her. She stopped and shook her head, her heart jumping in her chest, despite herself. "You didn't have to come all the way out here."

"I know, but the women in my family are worried about you. They want me to bring you back to the house for some lunch."

"I'm fine. My feelings were a little hurt, but I'll get over it. Sometimes you can't fix a problem, you just have to learn to live with it. My mom used to say that all the time." She grinned at him. "Not exactly Pollyanna, my mom."

"She was right, I think. Some problems you just have to survive, but we can help by letting everyone get to know you. Right now people are focused on the picture that Roy painted for them. We just need to give them a different, more realistic picture." He smiled, his mouth tipping up at the corner, and she couldn't help it.

She grabbed the sides of his face and laid one on him. His lips parted, probably in shock, under hers. She stepped back. "Wow. Sorry. I…"

He laughed. "I don't think I've ever had anyone feel the need to apologize for kissing me. I'm going over to the cabin to try to finish things up so Amelia and I can move in a couple days." He walked along the fence toward the barn as she walked along on the other side.

"Want some help? It could be fun to actually finish something."

"Yeah, you can help me haul the furniture I stored in the barn around the pond to the house." He looked hopeful.

She laughed. "Never mind, that doesn't sound like fun at all."

He slid the barn door all the way open and his

voice came from inside. "Too bad. You already volunteered. Let's start with the mattresses."

Two hours later, all the furniture was loaded in and Claire had collapsed on the front porch of Joe's cabin with a Diet Coke. The sun was setting over the pond and her muscles were once again aching from exertion. Between the bareback ride and moving Joe and Amelia's furniture into the cabin, she wouldn't be able to move tomorrow.

Joe dropped to the porch beside her. "Well, the furniture is in. The mice will enjoy it tonight."

She laughed and flopped back, too tired to even sit upright. "You know, Joe, the ceiling of the porch would be so cute if you painted it sky blue or sea-foam green."

"No." He didn't even let her finish. "I'm retired from painting. I have neon-green splotches on parts of me that should never be neon green. I get a headache every time I walk in my own bathroom. Never again."

"Mmm-hmm." She tucked that little idea for the ceiling away for some time in the future when her own projects were all done. "Amelia is going to freak when she sees all the furniture in there."

He yawned and hauled her to her feet before starting back to the main house. "I hope she likes it as much as she thought she would."

"With all the little touches you've put in there, I don't know how she couldn't. I know you didn't want flower-shaped lights in the bathroom, but she's going to love it. She deserves a little bit of childhood." She wobbled on a loose rock and he wrapped one long arm around her, rescuing her from a certain freezing cold bath in the pond. And after she was steady on her feet again, he didn't move it. Skin warmed, heart picked up, cheeks flushed, and she had to wonder if kissing him at the corral had been wise. She forced her train of thought back to whatever he was saying.

What was he saying?

"I'll bring her out tomorrow afternoon and we can make a list of stuff to buy. Maybe we can move in next week."

Though the secret wanted to burst out of her, she didn't tell him that she and his mother had made a list and all the "stuff," as he called it, was in the ballroom at her house waiting for the right moment to load it into the cabin. He and Amelia would be so surprised tomorrow afternoon after she and Bertie got through with the place.

He turned toward her when they reached his truck, his light blue eyes intent on hers. She had an almost irresistible urge to tidy her hair, which she knew had to be a flyaway mess after the ride through the pasture earlier.

"You're really something special, Claire." Joe skimmed his fingertips down the side of her face. "My timing has always been terrible. I wish things were different."

Claire wanted to pretend like she misunderstood him, but she didn't. Joe had a dream, too—returning to his team. And with the townspeople in an uproar and Amelia just coming into his life, it wasn't the right time for romance. She understood that.

But he was warm and solid and real and had such a heart to do the right thing. She was practical, but it was there—buried, but still—the wish that somehow the timing was different.

She sighed and smiled. "In some ways, the timing is perfect. We both just moved here. I like kids, you have one. We can be really great friends."

Joe nodded his head slowly, the regret evident in his eyes as he stepped back. "We are friends. Thanks for the help today, Claire. Don't let the turkeys get you down."

Tears pricked in her eyes. "I won't. Want me to pick Amelia up at school tomorrow?"

"I'm going to bring her out so I can see her

reaction when she sees the furniture in there. We're getting close."

"You are. It's a new start for the two of you."

He swung into his truck and rolled the window down. "See you tomorrow."

She stood there long after his taillights disappeared. She didn't need a man in her life, not now. She was rebuilding this place to provide a home and a family for kids. Everyone deserved a place where they belonged.

Maybe she was falling for Joe, but wishing she belonged with him would only make her own loneliness more pronounced.

She started for the barn to feed the animals but dug her cell phone out of her pocket and dialed Bertie as she walked. "Hey! He just left. Want to come over?"

A few hours later, Joe cautiously approached the front porch of his cabin to retrieve the wallet he'd left there earlier. He'd noticed his mother's car parked at Claire's and was slightly afraid of what he might find inside. Pushing the door open slightly, he stopped and gaped. The room he and Claire had left with a few pieces of random furniture had been transformed into a cozy, family-friendly retreat. "What...?"

"Joe!" Claire jumped to her feet from the

couch where she was sharing a Coke with his mom. "Um...surprise?"

Mom didn't move, just sat there with a satisfied smile on her face.

He didn't know what to say, so instead he looked around at the unbelievable change that had taken place here. Lamps on the end tables threw warm light across the blue velvet hand-me-down couch. Small candles were placed on the mantel and the coffee table. A fuzzy lime-green blanket was tossed across the back of the couch but still somehow looked artful.

Incredulous, he turned toward the kitchen. Neat stacks of white plates, cups and bowls lined the open shelves he'd exchanged for the falling-down upper cabinets. A wooden bowl on the island held a selection of limes, repeating the color from the throw on the couch.

"Joe?" Claire was starting to sound a little worried.

He smiled and then caught sight of the back wall of the living room, and his breath left his chest. Pictures of him and pictures of Amelia had been framed and hung. The center of the grouping was a large photo of the two of them, heads together over the little kitten that Amelia had adopted. He hadn't even known Claire was taking it.

Turning to these two women who had managed to pull one over on him, he shook his head. "I don't know what to do with you two. You've made a home for me to bring my daughter to. There's not a thank-you big enough for this."

From the couch, his mother said, "My legs are too tired to stand up or I would show you, but you should look at the bedrooms, too."

He wasn't sure how it could top the transformation in the living space, but somehow it did. Where before there had been bare mattresses and floors, now there were bedspreads and pillows and comfortable-looking things. His room was a haven of masculinity. Dark colors, simple lighting. A leather pillow on the bed made him laugh. Amelia's bedroom was an explosion of pink. Her throw pillow was made of lavender feathers. Perfect.

"We let Amelia pick out her bedding. We figured it would be important to her," Claire said from behind him. "I hope we didn't overstep."

He laughed. "If you only knew how much I've been dreading shopping for all this stuff."

"We kind of figured. There's drinks in the fridge and some basic groceries in the pantry."

"I really don't know how to thank you." He followed Claire the few steps back into the living room.

"You don't have to. It was our pleasure. Plus, when you move, I'm making the pink room my office." She winked at Mom and walked toward the door. "I've gotta run, though. We weren't planning the reveal until tomorrow, so I'm glad we were finished when you came back!"

"I just can't believe this place. Thank you, Claire."

She nodded. "It was fun. Bye, Bertie."

Joe turned back to his mother. "You two are crazy."

"I'm crazy. That pretty young woman is crazy about you." She raised one eyebrow, but her customary sass was nowhere to be seen. She was serious.

He shook his head. "I don't know about that, Mom. I think maybe she's like that with everyone. But you, you're amazing. How did you keep this a secret?"

"A mother never tells her tricks of the trade, darling."

He walked his mom to her car and held the door for her. "I'll be right behind you."

Glancing at the brightly lit windows of Claire's house, he remembered what his mother said. He wanted to dismiss the thought, but truthfully, he worried about it. He liked Claire—liked her enough to be interested in pursuing this thing and that hadn't happened in a while.

They had created a home for him and Amelia. Claire was building a life here. His life was in Florida with his team. It just wasn't fair to pretend that they could have a future.

Chapter Ten

Claire tossed another sheaf of papers into the fireplace, the crackling fire making her remodeled kitchen into a cozy haven against the chilly November night. After the workers left for the day, she'd made herself a peanut butter sandwich and a cup of hot chocolate and changed into her yoga pants so she could get to work on a project she'd been purposely avoiding.

Tomorrow a nice soft sage green was going on the walls of the second-floor office. She'd been dreading going through her father's papers, but the painters had to be able to actually get in the room in order to paint it. She couldn't put it off anymore. So she'd put on some music on her iPod and resolved to just get through it.

She'd gone through two stacks of boxes already, hauling them into the kitchen and sorting through them. A couple of gems had been tucked away in those filing boxes, like some old maps of the area. Black-and-white photographs of the town were hiding in there, too, and would look great in the long upstairs hall. She flipped through the files, which appeared to be more papers from her father's time as mayor and an ill-fated run for governor. She pulled those out, throwing them with the others on the fire. When she went back for the next handful, her eye caught on a file that was titled, simply, GIRLS.

Heart pounding in her chest, she pulled out the file and sat down in the huge chair in front of the fireplace, legs crisscrossed underneath her. A manila envelope fell out into her lap. With trembling fingers, she unfastened the closure and opened it, first pulling out a hospital bracelet the width of no more than two of her fingers. It was joined by a tiny cap and a card with *Baby Girl 1* written on it, and beside it, in pencil, *Claire*. She'd weighed seven pounds four ounces and had been twenty inches long.

When she flipped it over, she saw two itty-bitty footprints—her footprints. A tear dropped, quickly seeping into the old card. She'd never seen anything from her birth, never even heard the story until her father's attorney told them the story about their biological mother's death from an aneurism when they were newborns. Her father hadn't felt like he could raise twin girls on his own, but he had wanted to find them as adults.

The attorney said it took two years for a private investigator to track her and Jordan. He'd traced them through the foster-adoption agency, pulling threads until he'd found their mom and ultimately the two of them. They met their father for a few brief hours one weekend, with plans for another visit, but by then their father had passed and their opportunity to hear their story firsthand was lost.

She placed the items gently on the table beside her, adding Jordan's to the small pile. Next out of the file was a letter-sized envelope that held old photos. In the first one, a woman in a hospital bed held a baby. On the back it said, *Anna with Claire.* The pang of grief surprised her. It was strange, she thought, to feel the loss of a person she had never known, to see a glimpse of what her life might have been like if she hadn't been adopted.

She set the photo aside and pulled out one of her and Jordan together—tiny babies dressed in pink. Her biological father was holding one on each arm with a big grin on his face.

Her breath stopped. In this picture, he looked like a proud papa. He looked like any other young father, equal parts joy and fear. She ran a finger down the faded face in the picture. *I wish I'd known you.*

She took a photo with her phone and texted it to Jordan. About four seconds later, the phone rang. She smiled. "Hey."

"What is that?" Jordan's voice demanded info, now. She never had been one to be particularly patient. Maybe that came with the red hair.

"It's you and me with our father."

Silence. Then, "He doesn't look like a father about to give up his babies."

Claire sifted through the photos again, pulling out one of their mother when she was obviously pregnant, their father standing at her side. "I guess maybe she hadn't died yet. There are some pictures with her in them, too."

"Our mother? What does she look like? Wait, no. Is that, like, dishonoring Mom to want to know?"

"No. I don't think Mom would care. She always said that she would support us trying to find our biological family if we ever wanted to."

"Okay, so what does she look like?"

"She has your red hair and my eyes." It was eerie, actually, to see their features in someone else's face. They'd never had that experience growing up. "She's really beautiful, like you. I'll send you one."

Jordan was quiet for a moment. "Maybe he loved us, Claire. Maybe the house was a real gesture of love rather than just a guilt thing."

Claire walked to the window, looked out over the field and imagined her father had stood in this exact spot. Instead of the normal tension of a memory of the man she'd never met, she felt a connection, something shared with the father who gave her life—twice, once through birth and once through adoption. "Maybe he did the only thing he thought he could do. I wouldn't trade our life with Mom for anything. We wouldn't be the same people if we hadn't been adopted."

"No, I wouldn't change anything, either." Jordan paused. "It's weird, Claire. Knowing this about him doesn't really change anything for us, but somehow I feel like everything is different."

As usual, her twin's words echoed her thoughts. "Me, too, J."

She heard muffled voices, then Jordan's voice came on the line again. "I've got to run. Someone's here to look at Sugar. If they buy him, Hot Rod will be the only horse left to sell."

"Hey, Jordan? I love you."

"Love you, too. I'll talk to you tomorrow."

Claire hung up the phone as Joe's truck pulled into its usual parking spot by the path to the cabin. Amelia tumbled out, hefting her backpack to her shoulder. Claire could see her lips moving a mile a minute. She laughed, imagining how excited Amelia was about seeing the finished cabin for herself.

Joe closed the door to the truck and glanced up at the window. She knew when he caught sight of her because a slow grin spread across his face. She took a deep breath as her heart rate picked up. Waggling her fingers at him, she returned the smile.

Amelia must have called to him, because he said something toward the cabin and started that direction, turning back to wave at her one more time.

He was really a good man. A good father, learning and growing every day. She glanced down at the picture she held of her own father and for the first time, maybe ever, she thought he might've been a good father, too. Maybe he made a mistake stepping out of their lives, but he didn't do it because it made his life easier, at least she didn't think so now. He did it because he thought it was what would be best for her and Jordan.

She imagined Joe and Amelia looking in

all the nooks and crannies of their cabin, discovering the surprises that she and Bertie had hidden for them. She was discovering things, too, definitely about her biological family, but she was also learning things about herself and the future she wanted to create.

The lights flashed on in the kitchen across the pond. At least a small part of her wished that Joe could be a part of that future. She went back to the files, pausing a moment with the picture of a man with two baby girls. Sometimes things didn't exactly turn out the way you planned or imagined.

And sometimes God had bigger things in store.

Joe backed into the gritty cinder brick wall, that feeling churning in his gut that something wasn't right. Tendrils of fog swirled around his ankles, silence heavy, the night air damp this close to the ocean. He caught True's eye and motioned for True to search to his left.

Leading with his weapon, True turned into the narrow passageway. They were searching for the perpetrator from a robbery earlier in the day. An anonymous tip led them to the docks, where a string of alleys connected warehouses and businesses that had long pulled out of this declining neighborhood.

Joe took another careful step and stopped as the hair prickled on the back of his neck. He scanned the dark windows above their heads.

No sign of movement—but something gnawed at him. He fought the urge to hold his breath until the dim light illuminated True as he stepped back into the alley. Joe took one step toward him. Just one lousy step.

The bullets came from the rooftop, as they always did, slicing right into the space where his vest met his armpit. Poker-hot pain arced into his chest and his legs refused to work. He looked at True, whose face erupted in rage as he shouted into his mic, "Shots fired, shots fired! Officer down! I repeat, officer down."

In slow motion, the sound faded into static and his eyes rolled toward the sky. His body fell, even though he wanted to stay on his feet. Every cell in his body strained toward consciousness. His vision grayed.

"Show me your hands. Down on the ground. SBPD. Get down on the ground." The sound of his team taking the shooter into custody.

Cold flooded his body, but it didn't hurt now. Rapid-fire thoughts converged into a single one: breathe.

He jolted awake as his body slammed into the hardwood floor. Sweaty and shaken, he stared at the ceiling as it slowly came into focus. Freshly painted beadboard. Ceiling fan. His new bedroom in the cabin. And with that recognition came the knowledge that the breathlessness was the dream, not reality.

"Dad!" Amelia dropped to her knees at his side, terror at being woken up out of a deep sleep in her eyes. "Dad, are you okay? I heard yelling."

He pushed up on one elbow. His skin was clammy and he was still quaking inside. "I'm fine, kiddo. Just a bad dream. Come on, I'll tuck you back into bed."

She looked at him like maybe he'd grown a third head, but she stood up as he gingerly got to his feet, rolling his shoulder.

The front door burst open. "Joe? Amelia!"

Joe grabbed a T-shirt off the end of the bed and jerked it over his head and wished like all get-out that he could just disappear right now. "We're in here."

Claire's head popped around the corner. "Are you okay? I heard shouting."

"We're fine. I had a bad dream, but we're fine. I'm going to tuck Amelia back in bed and I'll be right out."

Joe followed Amelia into her room, a rosy glow filling the room from all the pink, down to the night-light. Even her nightgown was pink, picked out by her grandmother. He smiled to reassure his daughter and pulled the covers up to her chin. "Sorry I woke you, pumpkin. Try to get some rest, okay?"

"Okay, Joe. I love you." Her eyes were already drifting shut. At her words it was like his whole world slowed to a stop, his heart stuttering before it picked up the beat again. She'd been in his life only a few weeks and she was his whole world.

He brushed her hair away from her face with a hand that was far too rough to be touching her. "I love you, too, Amelia."

Claire had tea made when he walked into the front room. He didn't know they had tea. Or mugs, for that matter. But he took one and sat on a stool and leaned on the counter, letting the heat seep into his hands and ground him.

"Are you really okay?" she asked as she slid into the seat next to him. She wore pajama pants, a sweatshirt and flip-flops, her hair in a high ponytail, no makeup. She looked young and beautiful. All the things the story he was about to tell her was not.

"I should've realized I would dream tonight. I have it when I sleep somewhere new. It's more of a flashback, really, than a dream. Crystal clear. I'm walking down the alley and True—my partner—is in front of me and I know something is about to happen and I can't figure out what. And then I'm shot and trying to breathe."

She reached for his hand. "What kind of case were you working?"

"Fugitive apprehension. We got a tip he was down in the warehouse district. He was there. He shot me and True shot him. He was the unlucky one. True doesn't miss." His jaw slid forward, and as a distraction, he brought the cup to his lips and drank.

"I'm sorry. That must've been awful." Her eyes were soft and she smelled like fresh apples, which shouldn't be that appealing but was, and he didn't think, just reached for her. His hand slid into her hair, freeing it, and he drew her close. He lingered and then gently touched his lips to hers.

He let himself sink. Into her sweetness, honesty and optimism. Only for a moment, but he needed this, needed her. Her breath rushed out in a little sigh and he let his forehead touch hers. "You're just so...perfect."

Like the springs the town was named for, she was a fresh infusion of pure joy. Red Hill Springs didn't know it yet, but like the springs to the settlers all those years ago, she was just what they all needed.

She laughed, but her eyes were wide, her

cheeks a little flushed. "Either you're very okay or you've completely lost your mind."

He slid his hand down her arm to cup her elbow and watched as her skin prickled. He wasn't the only one feeling with a heightened sense of awareness. "Probably a little of both," he admitted.

"How'd you get that scar by your eye?" She touched it gently.

"I got that one in Iraq. It bought me a trip home and a couple months in Walter Reed. The vision came back and it doesn't hurt, but my eyes are really sensitive to light, which is why I wear those cool sunglasses."

She pulled up her sweatshirt and showed him a scar on her lower abdomen. "Appendicitis. Senior year. I missed the prom."

He showed her his elbow. "Bike wipeout on the asphalt. I was ten, cutting school."

Claire pulled her hair away from her forehead to reveal a tiny scar. "Got kicked trying to milk a goat."

He rubbed his thumb over the inside of her elbow. "What about these?"

She went still. Her face was down, a curtain of hair hiding her expression. Finally, she said, "I used to cut myself. As a teenager. I was kind of messed up for a while about being put up for adoption by my biological parents. I had this idea that if I wasn't good enough for my own parents, how could anyone else want me?"

"Oh, Claire." He didn't know what to say. She was so far from not being good enough. "It was his loss. He had no idea what he missed."

"I know. I think he was doing the best he could at the time. And I don't have those feelings—much—anymore." She pointed to her hip. "I have a huge one there from softball. Sliding into home."

"Hangnail." He held out his thumb and she kissed it. The smile faded from his face. "You really are special. I hope you know that."

"I'm not, Joe. I'm just a regular girl." Sliding off the chair, Claire shook her head. "It's late and we both have a lot to do tomorrow. Look, it was an emotional night. It doesn't have to mean anything if you don't want it to."

Her eyes were big and dark in the dim room, the only light from a small table lamp in the living area. He was so tired. He didn't even pretend to not know what she was talking about.

"Did it mean something to you, Claire?"

She stopped halfway through the door, looked back at him. Slowly nodded. "It meant something."

As he watched her walk back to her house

in the moonlight, he knew it meant something to him, too. But he wasn't sure what he could possibly do about it.

Chapter Eleven

Claire put a cup of milk on the island in front of Amelia. "Drink up. And make sure you tell your dad milk is healthy."

"Do I tell him I drank it with cookies?"

"Those have oatmeal, pipsqueak. Oatmeal is a whole grain. Whole grain is healthy. Therefore, these cookies are healthy."

Amelia laughed and nibbled at another cookie, trying to pretend she wasn't really watching the road for her dad.

Claire climbed back onto the stool at the other end of the island. The bills she'd been poring over stared at her, their black-and-white print glaring.

When she felt the panic begin to rise, she reminded herself, *Whoever has God lacks nothing. God alone is enough.* It was truth, plain and simple, but she had to wonder if Saint Teresa of Avila had ever tried to renovate a two-hundred-year-old plantation home on a budget.

Claire looked out the window, away from the ledger that just seemed to laugh at her and her rapidly shrinking reno fund. There was a storm brewing, dark gray clouds stacking on the horizon. She tried to reassure Amelia. "I'm sure he'll be here soon."

But inside, she was jumpy, too. Waiting for Joe.

At the sound of tires crunching on the gravel drive, Amelia shot like a rocket out the back door to meet her dad at his truck. Claire followed a little more slowly, wondering at the little thrill of excitement in her own stomach. He was her friend, her tenant. And the guy she'd kissed in the front room of that cabin, her jumpy stomach reminded her.

He grabbed Amelia up into a whirling hug before depositing her back on the ground with a kiss on the head.

"Come on, Joe. Claire made cookies. Like actually made them with flour and stuff." She caught herself and cut her eyes up at her dad, before grinning at Claire. "They have healthy things in them."

"Healthy cookies?"

He shot Claire a look over Amelia's head and she shrugged. "Oatmeal. It's healthy."

As she walked back toward the house, Claire squinted at layer upon layer of brooding, jaggy-edged clouds. The air felt heavy and warm. Not Novemberish at all. Despite the mild temperature, she shivered.

"I could definitely use a cookie." Joe's smile was warm but tired. He followed Claire and Amelia into the kitchen and whistled. "The kitchen looks great. I can't believe they finished it already."

"There might have been bribing involved."

He arched a brow over one icy-blue eye. "Local law enforcement does not take kindly to bribery. Or so I hear."

"No laws broken. I bribe with cookies and the occasional hamburger from the Hilltop. Mostly everyone is just working really hard. I think they all understand that I have a limited time to get all the reno done."

He munched on a cookie. "Wow, these are good for health food. Is the rest of the house this close to being finished?"

"The whole bottom floor looks really good. I have an actual bedroom now. And the dining room is ready to be a dining room or study room or playroom or whatever we decide it will be."

"And you have a bathroom?"

"Four. And they all have plumbing that

works now." She grinned and looked out the window at the trees swaying in the gusting wind and wondered if she should check the weather.

"Good to know. Plumbing is important. What about the ballroom?"

"Nothing much has changed in there. When we finish the necessary updates, maybe we can give the wood some shine. I figure the kids who live here will be in roller-skating paradise in there until I decide what to do with it."

Amelia breathed out a gasp. "For real? How about the neighbor kid?"

Claire laughed, gave Amelia a light shove and was rewarded with a sassy grin. "Of course, the neighbor kid. I thought that went without saying. There's so much left to do. Jordan will be here next week with the horses, so now I've got to get busy in the barn. The painters aren't finished upstairs, the roof still has to be fixed and no one has touched the third floor at all, except for prep. And also next week, the foster care licensing worker is coming out for our initial interview and home check."

"Are you nervous?"

"Not really." She brushed an invisible piece of dust off the gleaming marble surface of the island. "Okay, yes. A lot. I know we won't be finished with the renovations, but I want her to be able to see how great it will be in the end."

Amelia backed toward the door, a cookie in each hand. "I'm going out to say good-night to Freckles. I'll meet you at the cabin, Joe."

"It looks like a storm is blowing up, so keep an eye out." The door slammed on his words. He laughed, and as Amelia ran for the barn, ponytail swinging, he turned to Claire. "You'll be fine. The licensing person's going to love you and this place is amazing. What kid wouldn't want to live here?"

"I hope so."

"The specialist I saw today said he thought it was possible that I could get full function back in my hand."

"Oh, Joe, that's great." And it was, but the idea of him leaving left her reeling.

"Well, I'd better go make sure Amelia's getting started on her homework." He stood but didn't move toward the door. Instead, he slid his hand into Claire's hair and pulled her in for a kiss that left her knees buckling and her brain scrambled.

"I've been wanting to do that since I walked in the door." His eyes searched hers, the corner of his mouth just tipping up, the half smile making her heart race. "I know it doesn't make sense, but when I'm around you, it doesn't seem to matter."

Claire opened her mouth to answer. Instead, the window over the sink shattered and she screamed. Joe dragged her to the floor, his hard, heavy body protecting her from danger. Wind and rain rushed in, wet leaves swirling to the floor around them.

He lifted his head, his icy-blue eyes laser-focused on hers. "Are you okay?"

"I think so." Her forehead was stinging. She reached up and brought her hand away covered in blood.

Sitting up, his back against the island, Joe dug his cell phone out of his back pocket, glancing at the screen and back at her. "Tornado warning. I need to get Amelia. Go to the storage space under the stairs and stay there until this is over."

"No, don't worry about me. I'll check the cabin and you check the barn. Faster that way."

He paused, clearly arguing with himself about sending her into danger. Finally, he nodded. "If she's not there, come straight back to the house and get under the stairs."

"Okay." She took a deep shaky breath. There were so many things that she wanted to say before they went out into the storm, but she wouldn't. They didn't need any distractions.

He gripped the door handle. "See you back here in a minute."

She nodded. He wrenched the door open and bolted into the storm. She didn't hesitate but lowered her head and ran for the cabin, heart in her throat.

"Amelia? Amelia!" Behind her, she could hear Joe echoing her words.

Above her, the clouds were boiling, the sky a sickly green color. Raindrops pelted her skin, soaking her clothes in less than a minute. Fear driving her, she ran faster, onto the porch, and threw open the door of the small cabin. "Amelia?"

The cabin was dark and still. No damage here. And no Amelia.

She quickly checked the bedrooms and bath, even looking under the bed. No sign Amelia had been here in the last few minutes. She must still be in the barn. After one last look around, Claire ran for the front door.

She slammed the door closed, casting a look at the ominous sky. She prayed for Joe to hurry. They should've been in a safe place a long time ago.

The barn door wouldn't budge. Joe struggled to open it even inches, until the wind snatched it from his hand and threw it back against the outside wall. He fell forward into the dim barn.

"Dad!" Amelia ran out of the shadows to him, words tumbling one over the other on a sob. "I was so scared. I got Freckles in his stall and was about to come back to the house, but I heard the glass breaking and I knew I couldn't."

He wrapped his arms around her and held her tight for a few seconds. "Okay, let's go. The house is still the safest place for us right now."

"I'm not— I can't."

"What do you mean, you can't?"

"Freckles is big, but he's scared. And the twins are in here, too. They're just babies." She had to shout over the noise of the rain lashing against the building.

"Amelia—" He was tempted to pick her up and put her over his shoulder. She was slight enough that, despite his injury, he wouldn't even break a sweat. But what would that prove? That the things that were important to her weren't important to her dad?

Something told him that this was a moment, one of those moments. The ones that your kids remember forever. Where Dad was either a hero or a gigantic jerk. He really didn't want to be remembered by his daughter as a gigantic jerk. Of course, he also wanted her to be alive to have memories.

He got on his knees in front of her, gripping her skinny arms. She felt so fragile in his big hands. "Listen, sweetheart. Whatever happens is going to happen, whether you are here or in the house. You can't stay here. It's not safe. I know you're worried about Freckles and Tink and the twins, so I think before we go, we should pray."

Tears were running down her face, mingling with her runny nose, but she nodded and sobbed, "Okay."

He grabbed her close. "Dear God, Freckles and Peter and Wendy and Tink belong to you. We leave them in Your hands and trust You to take care of them. Help them not to be scared. Keep us all safe. In Jesus's name, Amen."

Tipping her chin up, he said, "Ready now?"

She shook her head and grabbed his hand. "Just one more thing."

Joe sighed as she pulled him to the back of the barn. In the stall, the kittens were huddled in a bunch with Mama Kitty nowhere to be seen.

"Please, Dad?"

He didn't have time to argue. He nodded, falling to his knees and picking up the little babies. "Okay, let's go."

In the distance, the storm roared. They were out of time.

He grabbed his daughter's hand and ran.

Trees bowed in the wind, the storm rushing around them, bearing down on them.

"Dad!" Terror laced Amelia's voice. At the stairs, she tripped. He lifted her to her feet, slid his arm around her waist and tossed her to the top landing. "Go to the stairs!"

She ran through the open door, skidding on the wet kitchen floor into the hall. Claire scrambled into the hall, grabbed Amelia and pulled her into the storage area. He slid into the hall behind her, dived into the small space and pulled the door closed behind him.

Tears tracked down Claire's face, wet hair in ropes down her back. "I was so scared. I can't believe y'all made it in here." She held Amelia close, the light from her flashlight tracking wildly on the ceiling.

The old house shook and Amelia backed farther into the crescent of Claire's arm. "I've never seen weather like this."

Joe met Claire's worried eyes, before he smiled at his daughter. "I have. Our unit stayed during some of the hurricanes that hit northwest Florida. Don't worry, bug. This is the safest spot in the house."

At his words, the old house seemed to shift

and expand around them. He pulled his phone out of his back pocket and texted his mom, even though he knew it probably wouldn't go through.

"We're going to be fine." Claire rubbed a hand down Amelia's hair. She tilted her head, listening. "Wait. What's that noise?"

"Not the storm?" Joe asked, then laughed, relaxing just a little. He had a feeling he knew what she was asking about. He unbuttoned his shirt and, one by one, the kittens popped their heads out.

Claire burst out laughing and Amelia giggled, her eyes the exact mirror image of his own, shining.

"What's so funny?" he demanded. "Mama Kitty wasn't around. Someone had to take control of the situation."

One little tuxedo kitten tentatively picked his way across Joe's leg to curl up in Claire's lap. The roar of the winds had calmed outside, and tucked in their "shelter," they couldn't hear much at all anymore.

Claire scratched the little kitten's head. He could see the worry in her eyes. And he realized she worried for good reason. Her brand-new kitchen now held a few inches of rainwater and debris. They had no idea what was left of the rest of the farm or their town, for that matter. He prayed everyone was safe.

Overwhelming thanksgiving swamped him—that he, Amelia and Claire survived what had to be a tornado. Not knowing what might face them outside, a part of him wanted to stay cocooned in this tiny alcove for a long time. Instead, they would have to leave and take stock of the damage.

The faint sound of a siren reached them in their hidey-hole. The local first responders were riding the rural highways letting people know it was safe to come out. He picked up the kitten nearest him. "I'm going to take a look."

Amelia scrambled to her feet. "I'm going, too."

"Me, too." Claire passed one of the kittens to Amelia and picked the other two up from the floor. "I'm scared."

They walked down the hall to the kitchen, or what was left of it. Leaves floated on the rain-soaked floor. Half a tree was stuck in the kitchen window, dropping pine needles. Shards of glass sparkled everywhere. Amelia reached for Claire's hand.

Claire nodded. "Okay, we know there's going to be work here. Let's keep going. We need to check on the animals."

The back door hung slightly open, even

though Joe knew he had closed it. They stepped onto the porch and stood there, taking in the carnage. Small branches and leaves were scattered everywhere. On the highway, a power line sizzled and popped. Miraculously, the barn and their cabin still stood, although Joe could see that there were shingles missing from both structures.

A high-pitched whinny came from the barn. Claire ran for the barn and pulled the door open. "Freckles!"

"Is he okay?"

Claire rubbed her horse's neck. "I think he's fine. A little spooked."

"Tink?" Amelia ran to the last stall and peeked over the door. "They're all here." Her voice was thick with tears. "I was really worried about you guys."

He put his arm around Claire's shoulders, knowing how relieved she was but also how devastating this had to be for her. She had sunk every penny she had into this place and had already been worried about her finances and the timetable. She looked up at him. "We need to go check on everyone in town. I don't think the storm touched down here, but it might have in town."

Joe nodded. "I need to check on my mom and Jules."

"What about Mama Kitty?"

Claire drew Amelia into their small circle. "If she ran because she was scared, she's probably still hiding. We'll keep the kittens safe until she comes back."

He shifted the kitten he held to his other arm and dug his keys out of his pocket to unlock the door to his old truck.

"Oh, Joe, your truck." Claire's voice was dismayed.

It had a new dent in the roof from a limb, but he shrugged it off. "Just a scratch. It adds character."

"Is that what we're calling it?" his daughter muttered under her breath, but Joe made a face at her anyway.

"It's going to be a few days before the power is back on, especially if that system keeps moving east. I need to check on Mom and Jules while there's still daylight."

Amelia crawled into the backseat and pulled a small box from the floorboard. She shimmied out of her sweatshirt and arranged it into a makeshift bed for the kittens, collecting the ones that Joe and Claire were holding.

Claire opened the door and slid into the passenger seat. He looked at her, surprised. Her face pale but resolute, she sighed. "Nothing here is that urgent. It will all still be here tomorrow. Let's go check on everyone else. There may be someone who needs help."

It had been a crazy, terrifying, unbelievable day, but together they had survived. He could only pray that the town had fared as well.

Chapter Twelve

Trees snapped. Lines down. Debris scattered. Water standing. Everywhere Claire looked, she saw evidence of the storm's destruction. She closed her eyes, not knowing even what to say, just thanking God that they were safe. Her kitchen might be a shambles, but she and Joe and Amelia had not a scratch, and for a little while there, she hadn't been sure that would be the case.

Her eyes popped open as they bumped over a fallen branch, the limbs scratching the bottom of Joe's truck. He pulled into a parking spot at the Hilltop, where they could see others gathering inside. Claire followed Joe and Amelia into the café, looking around at the people, their faces reflecting the same shock and worry that Claire felt.

Bertie descended on them before the bell on

the door even stopped jingling. She grabbed Amelia's face in her hands. "Thank God you're okay. Was it bad out at the farm?"

"Not too bad." Claire was swept into Bertie's capable arms.

In his turn, Joe hugged his mom. "A tree branch came right in the kitchen window."

"Oh, Claire. Your beautiful new kitchen." Bertie's eyes filled with tears.

Claire shook her head. She didn't want to think about it, couldn't let herself think about it, or she would lose it. "It's just a kitchen. It's fine."

It *was* just a room, just stuff, but even as the thought passed her lips, she felt sick to her stomach. It represented so much work. So much money. It could be repaired, but her resources weren't limitless.

She shook off the thoughts. Joe and Amelia were safe. She was safe. People mattered most. "I'm just so thankful you're safe. Have you heard from Jules?"

"She's fine and the bakery is fine. I sent her home to check on the animals, but she should be back soon." Bertie poured a cup of coffee into the nearest waiting cup. "If you want to help, Joe, get into the kitchen and make some more coffee. We're going old-school without any power and using the gas stove."

"Yes, ma'am. I'm glad you're okay. Amelia?"

"I'll watch her," Claire interjected, before turning to Bertie. "Has everyone been accounted for in town?"

"That's a good question. I heard the bottom floor of the county hospital is flooded and the volunteer fire department was called in to help evacuate. Cops, too." Bertie talked as she walked, with Claire trailing behind her picking up empty cups and trash from the tables.

If all of the first responders were needed at the hospital, Claire wondered if there were people out there, like shut-ins, maybe, who needed help.

Joe came in from the kitchen door with a full pot of coffee. "Do you know if anyone checked on Mr. Haney?"

"I was just wondering the same thing." Claire nudged Amelia out of the way of the hot coffee.

Joe turned and let out a shrill whistle, quieting the room.

His deep voice carried throughout the diner without him even having to try. "Hey, anyone go down Haney Road to get here?"

There was a lot of muttering and looking around, but no one had been down the road where Harvey Haney lived. Claire put her hand on Joe's arm. "I think we should go check on him. If there's anyone else who is elderly or a shut-in, we can check on them, too."

"Amelia can stay here with me. I'll put her to work." Bertie looked around at the crowd of people. "I guess after that kind of storm everyone just wants a little bit of normal."

Joe pulled out his keys. "Thanks, Mom. If you think of anyone else who might need help, you can try to call me. Otherwise, we'll swing back by here when we leave Haney's place."

They drove down the highway taking the turn just before Claire's farm that led to Mr. Haney's cattle farm. The damage looked about the same as everywhere else, at least to Claire. "Maybe his phone is just out."

Joe swerved around a limb in the road. "Maybe. I'm worried about him, though. That storm blew up so fast, and if he was out in it, he could be hurt."

Claire looked out the window at the woods flashing by. The trees dripped water, some of their limbs bowed by the storm's lashing winds. She felt like the tree, a little battered, a little shell-shocked and storm-worn. Surely, soon things would start to fall into place and she would get her equilibrium again.

Claire gasped as a quarter of a mile out from Haney's house, the gently bowing trees turned into a scene of full-fledged destruction. The whole area looked like it had been bulldozed. The woodsy area had been decimated, leaving toothpick-like twigs, sticking up like a diorama forest.

As they rounded the curve nearest to the house, a black-and-white Holstein cow stood in the middle of the road. Joe slammed on the brakes, his arm shooting out to brace her.

The cow turned her head to look at them, then slowly ambled off the road.

"We'll come back for her. Let's go check on Mr. Haney first." Joe pulled into the driveway at Mr. Haney's ranch.

Claire swallowed hard. A tall pine tree had collapsed the roof of Mr. Haney's house, right through the center, and the barn was just... gone.

Joe slammed the truck to a halt in the driveway. He jumped out, leaving the keys swinging in the ignition, as he yelled for the older man. "Mr. Haney? It's Joe Sheehan. I helped you with the cows the other day, remember? Mr. Haney, are you here?"

"I'm going to see if I can find a way in."

His eyes were covered with his sunglasses, but she could see the worry on his face. "Be careful. We have no way of knowing how stable the house is."

Claire skirted the remains of the pine tree.

The garage door looked like it had buckled from the damage to the house. If she could get in, though, there was a good chance that the inside door wouldn't be locked.

The house was creepily quiet except for the occasional sound of the cows in the field. Claire stuck her head into the opening. "Mr. Haney?"

Nothing.

His car was in the garage. He used a golf cart these days to check on the cows, but she was pretty sure she could see the outline of it in the shadowy space. There was no doubt in her mind that he'd been home when the storm hit.

She was scared to go in, but there was no choice. Mr. Haney's life could depend on it. She stuck one foot in through the opening, calling back to Joe. "I'm going to try to get in through the garage."

"Let me go."

"No." She shook her head. "You won't fit through here. I'll call out if I see him."

Ducking down, she squeezed through the awkward opening and stopped to give her eyes time to adjust to the dim light. She edged around the big Buick that filled this side of the garage and put her hand on the doorknob to the house. It turned under her hand and she pushed it open.

The timbers that held the house together shifted above her. She froze. If it started to cave in, she could be trapped here, too. Her heart raced, but she wouldn't turn back, not until she searched what she could of the house.

She heard Joe calling from outside. "Claire!"

"I'm okay. I'm good." She took one tentative step forward and called out again. "Mr. Haney? It's Claire Conley. Remember me?"

The house settled again and she placed her hands on the wall, glancing at the ceiling as dust rained down. From beyond the kitchen, she heard a groan. Faint, but there.

She rushed forward, all thoughts of her own safety vanishing. Mr. Haney was in here and he needed their help.

Joe watched as Claire disappeared into the garage and fought a small war with himself about charging in after her, never mind that he wouldn't fit through the narrow space the crumpled door opened up. He wanted to keep her safe, never let anyone or anything hurt her.

And he didn't want to analyze that at all.

Instead, he thought about Mr. Haney as he walked around back to see if there was an easier way in. Mr. Haney had been the 4-H sponsor at the elementary school when Joe had attended. The now elderly man had known that Joe couldn't have an animal to take care of, not when he didn't even have food to eat himself. So Mr. Haney had invited Joe to come to the farm whenever he could and, though he'd never made a big deal out of it, he always seemed to have extra food when Joe came around.

A muffled shout came from inside the house. "He's here! Joe, I found him!"

Joe raced onto the back porch. The glass had burst out of the back window when the tree fell, pine branches protruding out. "Claire?"

"In here. Mr. Haney's breathing, but he's not responding."

Training kicked in, narrowing his focus to the next task he needed to accomplish in order to reach the desired outcome. He took off his flannel shirt and wrapped it around his hand and broke out what was left of the window framing so he could climb inside. Pushing through the remnants of the huge pine tree, he saw Claire, kneeling on the wet floor next to Harvey Haney's still body, her hands pressed on a wound on the old man's denim-clad thigh.

Joe pressed 911 on his phone, knowing if he did manage to get through that it might be a long time before anyone could reach them.

As the operator picked up, he saw Mr. Haney stir. Thank God.

He asked the operator for an ambulance, gave her the address and dropped to his knees beside Claire. "Is he conscious?"

"He's in and out. This cut on his thigh is the worst. It was still welling blood when I got in here. He's got a cut on his forehead, too, and his legs are pinned under the tree. It looks like it fell right where he was sitting."

"Keep pressure on that wound. I'll look around. I'm sure he has a first-aid kit in here somewhere."

"I just want him to be okay." Her eyes were big and dark in the shadows of the damaged house. In them he saw the heart that drew everyone to her, the compassion that pushed her to do things other people only thought about.

Joe wanted to reach out to her, reassure her everything was going to be fine. But it wasn't that simple. "I know. Me, too. We're going to do everything we can. Let's just try to keep him from moving around so he won't do any more damage."

He strode down the hall, the sagging ceiling dusting his hair with bits of plaster. The power was out from the storm, but they needed to cut the power off to the house before the situation became even more dangerous.

Opening the first door he came to, he found a bedroom. Furniture that would have been nice thirty years ago and a bed with a hand-made quilt. That looked like Mr. Haney. His barn was state-of-the-art, but his bedroom wasn't important as long as he had somewhere to sleep.

Joe walked through to the bathroom and found a first-aid kit under the sink. Grabbing the quilt from the foot of the bed, he hurried back to Claire's side.

Mr. Haney was fighting for consciousness. Joe placed a hand on each of Harvey's shoulders, gently keeping him in place, but the old farmer struggled against his hands.

Stroke-weakened muscles made it harder for him to talk, but he was whispering something. Joe leaned closer so he could hear. "Have to get up. Check on the stock."

"This is Joe, Mr. Haney. It's okay. The cows are taken care of."

His onetime mentor's shoulder eased under his hand. "You've always been a good boy, Joe. I told Chief Sheehan not to worry about what anyone in town thinks. You deserve a family."

"Thanks, Mr. Haney." His throat clamped down around the words. He tucked the warm quilt around Harvey's frail shoulders. "I think you're pretty special, too."

The elderly man squinted rheumy eyes at Claire. "Hazel, is that you, sweetheart? The storm was so bad. I was worried."

Claire's breath caught. She leaned over where he could see her and, with her free hand, gently brushed the hair away from Mr. Haney's battered face. "I'm here, Harvey. It was a bad storm, but I'm fine."

As the old farmer's body sagged in relief, a tear dripped down Claire's face before she quickly scrubbed it off and sniffed. "You're going to be okay, too, Harvey. Just close your eyes and rest for a minute."

The lines in Mr. Haney's craggy face eased. Joe placed his fingers on the side of his neck. "Pulse is a little weak, but there. He's a tough old guy." He unzipped the first-aid kit. "I don't know what all is in here, but… Oh, good. Here's some gauze."

"He really loved his wife."

"They were inseparable. She led the choir at church and he was an usher. Always had a pocket full of peppermints. And apparently, he had a hand in defending my parents' decision to adopt a troublemaker teenager." He handed several gauze pads to Claire, who used them to apply pressure.

"I don't think he saw you as a troublemaker. I know your mom and dad didn't see you that way. And they were right." Her eyes were bright still, tears clinging to her lower lashes. "Is that why you left Red Hill Springs? You felt like a delinquent still?"

He didn't answer. He didn't know the answer, really. Hadn't examined his motives in years. Or ever. Finally, he shrugged. "I don't know. Maybe. I guess I knew if I stayed here I'd always be fighting a losing battle to overcome where I came from—what I came from."

She took the roll of gauze he handed her and wound it tight over Mr. Haney's thigh. "I understand. It's hard to get past feelings that are so entrenched as children. I don't like that everyone knows my biological father gave me up for adoption. I fight feeling like I wasn't good enough for him then and not good enough for this town now. I think they're all talking about me and the conversation dies down when I walk into the room."

"They don't do that." When she snorted, he smiled and added, "Anymore. Hopefully, now that they're getting to know you, they're starting to see what an amazing person you are and what a great asset you will be for Red Hill Springs."

Her hands were gentle as she comforted Mr. Haney. "It was crazy, moving here without ever laying eyes on the place. I realize that. I just knew, I guess, if I never took a chance, that I would never know if I could do it. I wanted to quiet the voices in my head that said I wasn't good enough."

"I hope you know that you are." He lifted his head as sirens sounded in the distance. "Help is here, Mr. Haney, you did good. We're going to get you to the hospital so you can get back to taking care of your cows."

"Hazel?" Confused blue eyes met Claire's. "Are you coming with me?"

"I can't go in the ambulance, but I'll stay with you as long as I can."

Joe rolled to his feet and said quietly, "I'm going to meet them out front, but I'll be right back."

The firefighters were gearing up in the front lawn when Joe jogged around to the front of the house. He sent the EMTs around back and filled the firefighters in on how the tree had Mr. Haney trapped.

With the roar of chain saws and the choreography of a well-rehearsed group, the firefighters had the tree in pieces in minutes. A few minutes later, Mr. Haney was brought around the house on a gurney, an IV bag already dripping lifesaving fluids into his arm.

Claire's face was drawn and tired, but she kept her grip on Mr. Haney's hand. It had been a long afternoon. Joe met her at the ambulance door and leaned over to whisper in Mr. Haney's ear.

As the ambulance rolled away, he put his arm around Claire.

"What did you tell him?"

"Just that I would take care of things here. And I guess I need to go see about those cows."

Joe was halfway over the fence to the cow pasture when a car pulled into the driveway and four men got out, one settling a cowboy hat on his head. Mr. Campbell, the mayor. He stopped to talk to Claire, giving her a hug, before coming toward Joe, who had the presence of mind to slide off the fence as the mayor held out a hand.

Mayor Campbell's face held the worry and fatigue of a long, unpredictable day. "Thanks for coming out here to check on Harvey. We've been friends a long time, Harvey and me, and from what I heard from the firefighters, he might not have made it if y'all hadn't come out to check on him."

"I don't know about that, sir. But I'm glad we came out, too."

"Don't worry about the cows. Me and the boys here will take care of getting them back in the field and shoring up the fence."

Joe glanced back at the field and then nodded. "If you're sure, I'll take Claire home, then. She had some storm damage out at her place."

The mayor's gaze narrowed. "Bad?"

"Not like this, but bad enough to slow her progress down for a while. To be honest, we haven't had time to check it out."

"You go do that, then, and let me know if there's anything I can do to help." The mayor clapped a hand on Joe's shoulder. "I mean it now."

Joe watched the mayor's sons vault the fence into the cow pasture as the mayor himself walked back to his car. Maybe Joe had been right when he told Claire that public opinion was shifting. Maybe when the time came for the vote, it wouldn't be as bad as she thought.

And maybe those cows would fly back to the pasture on their own. Anything was possible. He slid into the driver's side of his truck and got a whiff of cat. "What the..."

Claire laughed. "We forgot about the kittens."

One tiny sharp-clawed feline, gray with white paws and chest, started its way up Joe's arm and Claire gently disentangled it. "This one likes you."

Joe scowled but took the fuzzy little cat and scratched its head. Doggone if the critter didn't start purring. He tucked it into the crook of his elbow and started the truck with a roar, giving Claire a sideways glance. "As long as it likes mice, we'll get along fine."

She laughed, relief palpable in the air. Mr. Haney was on the way to the hospital and thank You, Jesus, they had all survived.

It could've been worse. A lot worse.

Outside, the morning sun was glaring. Claire plugged the drill in to charge before she remembered that the power still hadn't been restored to the house. The kitchen, the room that yesterday morning had been such a bright spot—such a cheerful, grounding space—was dark. None of that beautiful early-morning light seeped in around the edge of the window she'd covered with plywood. Dirty water sloshed on the floor, the soggy, dirty mess reminding her what a failure this endeavor was turning out to be.

She'd risked everything to come here. Her biological father had left her this house and it had felt like a sign. *The* sign. The one that told her now was the time.

God had made a way for her to find out about her biological family, but more important, to make a home for difficult-to-place foster kids. Everyone was depending on her and what had she done? She'd totally screwed it up.

She scrubbed her hands over her face. Maybe the people in Red Hill Springs were right to be worried. Maybe she wasn't the person to make this dream happen.

A little dish beside the sink gleamed with a half dozen razor blades that she'd used to scrape the excess paint off the glass windowpanes. She'd hidden razor blades just like those in all kinds of weird places when she was cutting as a teenager. Back then, the pain she created on the outside made the massive hurt inside seem validated.

She ran her fingers over the thin silver-white scars on the inside of her elbow. The pain she'd felt as a teenager didn't make logical sense. She'd known that, even then. She'd had a loving mom, who adopted her and never made her feel like she was anything less than perfect. She and Jordan had been lucky.

But she couldn't explain the sense of loss she felt that her mom hadn't shared the same genes with her. Someone she could look at and say that's where my dimples, or my penchant for chocolate, or even my little toes that stuck out at a weird angle, came from.

That need to just be known created an ache inside that couldn't be soothed with a simple hug or a girls' night out with her mom. She had Jordan, thank God, but Jordan didn't know where those things came from, either.

It wasn't until a youth worker recognized Claire's silent scream for help and confronted her that she realized how dangerous a road she'd been traveling.

A tear slid down her cheek. She flipped the little blade in her fingers. At one time it had seemed like a friend. Now she knew it wasn't, but when the world felt out of control and she felt like that scared, confused teen…she'd be lying if she said she didn't think about it.

A knock jolted her. She stood completely still, letting the sounds of the farm bring her back to the present, to real life. Adult life. Her kitchen, someone at the door. She folded the razor blade, hiding it in her hand, and pulled the door open.

Chapter Thirteen

Joe stood on Claire's back porch in a battered leather coat he'd dug out of his dad's closet, collar turned up against the cold. He blew warm air into his cold fist and shuffled from foot to foot. That cold front driving the severe weather was no joke.

Claire pulled the door open. A huge sweat-shirt hung almost to the top of her bright red Hunter boots. She was such a dynamo, kick-dirt-take-names kind of person, but yesterday afternoon when they were pulling the tree out of her kitchen and covering the gaping hole with plywood, she'd seemed almost…fragile.

He was worried about her and wanted to check on her. She wouldn't go for that, so he made up an excuse, which also happened to be true. "I'm hoping you have some coffee on."

She pushed the door open wider. "I just made some in the French press. Help yourself."

"It's freezing in here. You don't want a fire?" He studied her face. She still wasn't right, her eyes huge and dark in her usually animated face.

"You can build one, if you want."

Joe crossed the soppy floor and took a piece of kindling out of the basket by the fireplace. "I called the hospital. Harvey's doing better. Mom said she talked to Harvey's daughter, Mary Pat, who just got a divorce. M.P. is thinking about bringing her kids and moving in with Harvey for a while. Could be good for both of them."

"That's great. I bet it will make him happy to have kids around."

He lit the kindling, tucked it under the logs and sat back on his heels. "So I got Amelia on the bus and I was walking back down the drive and couldn't figure out what was so weird. And then I realized, no trucks in the drive, no hammers, no people yelling over the sound of power tools."

She didn't say anything, just looked down at her clenched fist, her face still too pale.

Leaning closer to the struggling flame, Joe

blew gently until the logs started smoking and caught. "Where are the workers?"

Claire turned her back to him, walking through the smoke-hazy room to pour him a mug of coffee. "Don't make a big deal out of this," she warned.

She turned, her gaze anywhere but meeting his. "I sent them to Mr. Haney's this morning. When he gets out of the hospital, he needs a home to go back to."

He drank deeply from the mug she handed him, steam rising into the still chilly air. "You need them, Claire. Your licensing worker is coming next week."

"I know. Believe me. But Harvey needs them more." She shrugged like it didn't matter, but her voice wavered, her knuckles clenched white. He couldn't stand to see her like this. His jaw tightened.

When his hand touched her arm, she jumped. He cupped her fingers in his large calloused palm, gently uncurling them. "What is this?"

She closed her eyes. "I wasn't going to use it. I was just…holding it as a reminder not to give up. It reminds me where I came from and how hard I had to work to get here."

"And the storm made you question that?"

"No." She paused and he could see the emotion working on her face as she battled with what to tell him, if anything. "The failure did. We were on a tight deadline already and a strict budget and—" She gestured around the room and let her hand drop. "With all this, I'm not sure I'm going to be able to stick to my timeline."

He shook his head, trying to will her to see what was in his heart. "You're not a failure, Claire. Look at everything you've been able to accomplish in just a few short months. What a difference you've made for so many people."

He grazed his hand down her arm, stopping to cup her elbow in his work-roughened hand. "You're amazing, but even if— *even if*— you were an utter failure, you would be good enough. Mom used to tell me that so much when I was a kid that I muttered it in my sleep. She would say, even if you were the person you sometimes think you are, you are still enough." His eyes softened on hers. "God made you— knit you together cell by cell—and He doesn't make mistakes. You're here for a purpose and you're perfect for that purpose. I've seen it with my own two admittedly ugly eyes."

Claire's gaze locked on Joe's. "You make sense. And I know, in my head, that sending the workers over there was the right thing to do. I just don't know why it hurt so much to do it. Like I was giving up on my dream."

"You're so good at everything you do. No, you are," he said when she scoffed. "The animals, managing all the renovations, your rapport with kids, your junk food addiction."

When she laughed, he went for the win. "I'm not kidding when I say you're amazing. But being that good at everything sometimes makes hard things even harder because you're used to depending on yourself."

"Maybe you're right and all this is just about that scary place where pride and self-confidence meet. And maybe I need to trust that if this is God's plan, then He has it."

Her eyes held a little spark of life and he drew the first deep breath since he invited himself in.

She opened the door to the closet and pulled out a broom and a mop. "So, which one do you want?"

Claire snugged her gloves onto her hands and hefted the hay bale into place. It was so cold outside that Tink the goat had put one hoof outside the barn door and turned and gone back to her stall. The twins had no such compunction about the cold and were running in and out of the door, stopping randomly to butt heads and Claire's legs and pretty much anything else they saw. She smiled and shooed them out of the way.

The cold front that created a tornado when it went crashing into the warm moisture from the Gulf of Mexico apparently decided to stick around awhile. She'd slept in the keeping room next to the fireplace, dozing and tending the fire that Joe had built, until the power had sputtered back to life around three in the morning.

Joe slid the barn door open and stepped inside wearing boots and jeans and that beat-up leather coat. Somewhere he'd found a leather cowboy hat, and instead of looking silly on him, it just made him look dangerous. He grinned as one of the goat twins ran headlong into his leg. "Everyone stay warm and toasty last night?"

"Looks like it. This cold weather has Pete and Wendy feeling frisky. I, for one, was really glad to have the fire going last night. Reminded me of how things would've been in the old days." She tossed some hay into the trough outside. Freckles and Tink might be outside before she fed again this afternoon.

"No sign of Mama Kitty?"

"Nope." She dusted her hands and settled her hat. "I keep hoping she'll show up. Fortunately, the kittens are able to be weaned and are doing okay with the kitten food we picked up."

It had been a long, cold night and the kittens had slept curled up on the couch with her. The little gray-and-white one that Joe had claimed kept touching her face with his little cold nose, like he wanted her to wake up and do something.

She wished she knew what to do. Instead, she got up before the sun like she usually did and took care of feeding and watering the animals. Repetitive, yes, but the ritual was oddly comforting.

Car tires crunching on the driveway alerted her that someone was coming in. She narrowed her eyes against the bright early-morning sun. "Who's that?"

Before that car even got parked, a truck turned into her drive, followed by another car and an SUV. People poured out of the vehicles and into the yard. For a brief second, she wondered if they'd decided to go ahead and have the town meeting and kick her out now, while she was down.

But that was the pessimistic side of her, the side she didn't indulge. She pulled her gloves off and tucked them into her back pocket, climbing through the fence to cross the driveway.

"Hey, folks, what's up?"

Joe's friend from high school, Ellen, stepped

forward. "Well, Mrs. Bertie told us you had some damage and you wouldn't be able to have your inspection next week. We want to help."

She gestured to one of the men behind her. "Kevin here is a carpenter. He usually makes cabinets, but he's good with a saw. The rest of us aren't so handy, except maybe Ernest over there, but we figured we could use a paintbrush and a broom as well as anyone."

Claire didn't move. Her feet felt frozen in this spot. She was floored, absolutely floored, that they would come to help.

"Why?" The word strangled out over the lump in her throat. She cleared her throat and tried again. "Why would you do this?"

Mayor Campbell stepped out of the crowd. "You helped Harvey and you didn't have to. That's what neighbors do. We're your neighbors, Claire, even if we didn't act like it when you first got here. We're sorry about that and really just want to help."

A few people in the crowd nodded. She recognized so many of them, people she'd talked to or eaten with at the Hilltop. Some, like the young mom with the autistic son, had a vested interest in the place, but most were just being neighborly.

"So where do you want us to start?" Joe's

sister Jules held a bucket with paint supplies and Claire wanted to cry all over again.

Joe's voice from behind her startled her. "Where's your list, Claire? I know you have one or two or ten."

She grinned. "I don't know how to thank you, but I sure will put you to work. You may regret being so neighborly in the morning. The third floor needs to be cleaned and painted. The second floor is ready to be painted. The kitchen window was the worst damage."

The mayor sent a group of teenagers off with instructions to pick up limbs and pile them up. Ellen and a group of ladies went to the second floor to paint and Joe and Kevin were already deep in conversation about what to do about the window. Her phone buzzed in her back pocket. "Hello?"

"Claire, it's Bertie. I'm sending Ash out with some hot chocolate and coffee in a few minutes and I'll be out around lunchtime with some boxed lunches. Can you count up everyone for me?"

"I will. Bertie, was this your idea?"

"Honey, I don't know. Coulda been. But one thing I know, people jumped at the chance to help. And don't you worry about it. In Red Hill Springs, we might take our time coming around, but you're family now and family takes care of each other."

Claire had been searching for her family, like the biological kind, but she'd found a family in a whole different way.

"I've gotta run. I'll see you in a little while. Don't forget to text the number of lunches I need to make."

"Yes, ma'am." Claire sniffed back the tears, settled her hat and strode into the house. Her neighbors were inside working.

She had an inspection to get ready for.

As the sun dropped below the trees, the temperature dropped like a rock. Joe lit the wood that the kids had stacked up from underneath, a nest of newspaper the fire-starter. He stepped a few feet away and streamed some lighter fluid onto it. The limbs caught with a whoosh.

All afternoon, the ladies from the bereavement committee at church had been bringing casseroles, salads, plates of fried chicken and pans of lasagna. The older ladies set out the food, rapping hands as the teenagers nipped little tastes. Laughter rang in the air and Joe stepped back from the fire and just took it in for a moment.

Children careened around the back of the house, playing tag or horse race or whatever little kids played, their laughter and squeals echoing off the building. A more strident mom's voice cut through, warning them they better stay out of that pond. Amusement tugged the corner of his mouth up. Kids.

Jules and Amelia, with a little help from some of Amelia's school friends, hauled hay bales out around the fire in a big circle. When his sister put her arm around her niece and squeezed, his throat ached. He was just so grateful.

Disheveled and tired, paint-stained and dusty, the various workers trickled out of the antebellum plantation house and made their way through the food line, settling on the hay bales around the fire. He looked around for Claire but didn't see her, yet. And with a start, he realized his sunglasses weren't on his face. He patted his shirt pocket, but they weren't there, either.

He couldn't remember a time since his injury when he hadn't been completely conscious of where those glasses were at all times. His eyes were bothered by the light, yes, but his injured eye was a scarred mess and it bothered him that other people might be turned off by it.

Surprisingly, no one had run screaming. No one had even seemed to notice. Maybe the people who had seemed so judgmental weren't as judgmental as he thought. Maybe he was allowing his childhood insecurities to influence what he thought today.

He had no idea, but he should take some time to consider that since he had grown up and changed, maybe other people had done the same. Seemed like a no-brainer, but his insecurities had stalled him out somewhere around the age of fourteen, at least where it came to this town and its inhabitants.

As the crowd around the food thinned, he made his way to the back of the line. A voice behind him said, "Better not eat all that chicken."

He turned to find Mayor Campbell filling his own plate. "Mr. Mayor, I wouldn't think of it.

"Call me Chap, please. And if I may?"

"Of course. You've known me as Joe for a long time, sir." Joe handed the serving spoon for the corn-bread dressing to the mayor.

"Listen, Joe, this isn't really the time and place, but I'd like to talk to you sometime about applying for the job as chief of police. I did some checking into your record as a police officer and I believe we could use your kind of talent here in Red Hill Springs."

Joe blinked. Of all the things he might have imagined coming out of the mayor's mouth, that one never crossed his mind. "I...don't really know what to say. It's honestly something I never considered."

"Well, don't say no before we have a chance to talk. I just wanted to put a bug in your ear." Heaping a spoonful of green bean casserole onto his plate, Chap acted like he hadn't just dropped a bomb on the conversation.

Joe's hand still hovered over a dish of hash-brown casserole. The mayor nudged him. "Go on now. If you don't hurry, all those kids are going to eat Mabel's banana pudding before I get down there to get some."

"That would be a shame." Joe forced a smile. "Listen, sir, thank you for thinking of me, but…"

"You're planning to go back to your team. I understand. I just want a chance to sell you on staying here in Red Hill Springs."

As the mayor continued down the line, Joe remained riveted in his spot. Chief of police. Was he even interested in being the head cop in this little town, the town where he grew up? Maybe if he were, he could be more like his dad and less like Roy Willis. He could be good for the town.

His brother, Ash, had brought his guitar and was about halfway through a silly song about a hole in the bottom of the sea, sending the children, most of whom were his patients, into fits of laughter. Joe settled on a hay bale and had a mouthful of fried chicken when Claire settled beside him, her eyes glossy with tears.

She blinked away the wetness and a trembling smile spread across her face. "When I pictured what life could be like here, this is what I imagined. Bonfires and people everywhere, kids laughing, someone playing music. So much food. I keep wanting to pinch myself to make sure it's real."

"I didn't know that this kind of thing happened in real life. I thought it was just on television." He looked down at her sweet face lit by the firelight and wondered why he didn't just jump on the mayor's offer to apply for the chief of police job. He cared about her. His daughter was happy and settling in. His family was here, in more ways than one. But…

It always came down to the *but*. He loved his job. He was good at it in a way he had never been good at anything before. He made a difference. He loved the adrenaline rush. Thrived on it.

"Yesterday I thought my dreams for this place were through. But we're still here. We still go on. And we can trust that God is still in charge even when we don't understand it."

His brother, Ash, had switched from silly kid songs to worship music.

You make Beautiful Things out of the dust. Even the children were quiet when Jules joined in to harmonize on the chorus. *You make me new, you are making me new.*

Claire was openly weeping beside him. He put his arm around her and pulled her closer to him, whispering against her hair that it was all going to be okay.

His heart felt two sizes too big for his chest. How could he leave this? But how could he choose to stay knowing that his calling lay with his team in Florida?

Could God really take the chaos of his life lately and make something new out of it? Believing that, trusting that, would take faith that he wasn't sure he possessed. He glanced at the sky, stars scattered like a million tiny diamonds.

But maybe, it wasn't his faith that mattered.

Chapter Fourteen

The bells on the door jangled as Claire walked into Joe's sister Jules's bakery. She was instantly assaulted by the fragrance of bread baking, cinnamon and sugar and everything yummy.

"I've got your order right here, Claire. A dozen chocolate chip and a dozen of the thumbprint cookies. Those are my favorite." As she talked, Jules tucked two tiny cakes, each with a perfect pink rose on top, into a box and slid them into a bag. "My treat for when you rock your home study."

Claire grinned. "I wouldn't even be able to go through with it if everyone hadn't helped clean the place up."

"Mom said to tell you she's praying for you when she came in for her order for the diner this morning. Ellen and a couple of her friends came in for coffee and asked if we'd heard anything, too." Jules passed the box and small white bakery bag with her pink Take The Cake monogram over the glass case. "You should know by now that everything counts as news in Red Hill Springs."

"I'm starting to figure that out. But after the other night, I'm so grateful that it doesn't even bother me."

"I hadn't been in the plantation house since I was a teenager and sneaked in on a dare. It's a big old place, just crying out for a family. The former mayor and his wife never had kids." Jules paused midmotion. "Oh, Claire. I'm so sorry. I didn't even think before I said that."

"It's okay. He didn't have children that anyone knew about. Anyway, I hope there are lots more get-togethers at the farm. The other night was pretty special. You're invited to all of them, as long as you bring that carrot cake, like you did the other night." Claire pointed to the cooler and a magnificent five-layer monstrosity, defusing the awkward moment. It wasn't the first and surely wouldn't be the last.

"Deal. Now go, so you have time to put those cookies on a plate before your caseworker gets there." At Claire's blank look, Jules winked. "Never tell a guest you didn't make the treats. Southern-girl secret."

Ten minutes later, Claire was placing the last cookie on the plate when she heard a car in the drive. She started toward the front of the house, where no one but guests came to the door, stopping to adjust one of the daisies she'd picked up at the market yesterday. In a galvanized steel teapot, they were fresh and funky, traits she hoped this licensing worker could appreciate.

When the doorbell rang, she said another quick prayer, as if the never-ending litany of prayers she'd been saying for months wasn't enough. She nearly ran the length of the hall to the front door, stopped and smoothed her skirt down in the front. Taking a deep breath, she pulled the door open, a big smile on her face. "Hi, you must be Mrs. Rabun. I'm Claire Conley. It's so nice to meet you."

"Nice to meet you, too. Please call me Livvie." Mrs. Rabun—Livvie—stuck her quite large file under her arm and stepped into the house, her vision, like everyone's, drawn to the sweeping staircase. "What a beautiful old place."

"Thanks. We've been working hard to get it livable." Claire stepped aside for the caseworker, who didn't look anything like the matronly woman Claire had envisaged. Instead of a plump, grandmotherly figure with gray hair,

Livvie had on a long skirt and a peasant top accented with a variety of gold chains, charms and bracelets. Curly red hair formed a flyaway halo around her head.

"It's more than livable, it's lovely." She ran a finger down the glossy banister, her bangles jingling at the movement. "And you want to bring children in here? To scratch the floors and slide down this gorgeous banister?"

Claire grinned. "Yes. It's actually perfect for kids. Can I show you?"

"Yes, please."

She started on the third floor, with rooms she'd been able to prepare for kids yesterday because the volunteers had painted and cleaned and polished. The wide-open study area at the top of the stairs was perfect for teens.

On the second floor was Jordan's suite of rooms. Claire mentioned the plan for hippotherapy and showed off more bedrooms. No furniture yet in these rooms, but the walls had been painted vibrant kid-friendly colors. She showed the worker the ballroom and her suite of rooms, with the small attached office. The kitchen was last, with its enormous island and many stools, just waiting to be filled.

A cozy fire at one end, a brand-new window filtering golden light at the other, the room was once again perfect. Claire turned to Livvie with a smile. "That's it for the tour. There will be more furniture, of course. And outside, the animals and a garden, which the children who live here will hopefully learn to be responsible for. I want to give them a sense of belonging and pride."

Livvie scooched onto a stool and reached for a cookie. "May I?"

"Of course." Claire poured a couple cups of coffee and sat around the corner of the island from her caseworker.

"Claire, I don't have anything to argue with at all about the property and the job you've done renovating it. It's amazing." She opened her file and ran her finger down a list. "Your training will transfer and I have most of your forms on file now, but I'll need your new proof of insurance and notes from your veterinarian on the animals and whether they are fully vaccinated. Do you vaccinate horses?" She wondered out loud.

"Yes," Claire put in.

"Of course, that makes sense." Livvie, bracelets jangling, slid a form across the stainless-steel top of the island. "Here's a checklist. When I come next time, I'll check water temperature—under 120 degrees—and smoke alarms, one within three feet of each bedroom. You'll need to have childproof locks on any cleaning supplies and a locked cabinet for medications." She paused, looking over her notes.

Claire pulled out her own notebook. "I'm taking care of the last things on the checklist tomorrow. I want everything in order as soon as possible. Oh, and I should mention that I have a tenant in a small cabin on the property. He's a police officer recovering from an injury. His twelve-year-old daughter lives with him."

The resource worker glanced up. "And y'all are just friends? Romantic? Landlord and tenant?"

"Friends," Claire said firmly. And then wondered at the pang she felt in her chest. Were they friends? More? He meant something to her, something special. The image of the kiss they'd shared in the cabin popped into her mind. Her face flushed with heat.

Livvie gave her a speculative look over the top of her hot-pink reading glasses. "Well, if you become more than friends, update it with us, and he'll have to get background-checked, regardless. It may seem silly since he's a police officer, but it's policy."

"Got it. Thanks." Claire picked up the very long list of things the department needed in order to license her home. She'd made a lot of progress. She was so close.

The thought thrilled and terrified her. She knew a lot about being a foster parent because of her job as a caseworker, but she'd never had the sole responsibility of caring for them before, especially while owning a property and maintaining it.

Livvie closed her notebook. "There's one more thing I need to talk about with you. I got a call yesterday from the chief of police here in Red Hill Springs. He said he had some concerns about you being licensed for foster care."

Claire went still, her heart beating so loud she was sure that Livvie could hear it. Because it seemed that the town was more supportive of her, apparently Roy had turned to a more underhanded way of stalling out her plans. She cleared her throat. "What exactly were his concerns?"

"There were a couple of things that were also very concerning to me. The first was that you were arrested in your former hometown? He suggested that you moved here because of that arrest."

Claire's heart sank. "That's not true at all. When I was fourteen, I was picked up with a friend who was shoplifting and taken to the police station. I was questioned and released to my mom a few hours later. There was no arrest, but I was grounded for what seemed like forever."

"What did spur you into moving here?" Livvie's pencil was poised above her writing pad.

Claire took a deep breath. "There was no single driving force. My sister and I spent some time in foster care before we were adopted after our first adoptive placement fell through. I was a caseworker for children's services in Charlotte. The real catalyst for change, though, was that my mom died. I didn't really have anything holding me there. When my biological father left my sister and me this house, it seemed like the right time to take it on."

"I see. Well, it seems like the police chief was making a big deal out of something that was a long time ago. I would be more concerned if it seemed like there was a pattern, but still." The licensing worker didn't smile.

Panic started to bubble up in Claire's stomach. "Look, I'm not going to pretend that I was a perfect teenager. I wasn't. I was confused and hurting and did some stuff that I'm not proud of. But those same experiences give me insight into the kids who will come through here."

Livvie pursed her lips. "You're going to need the support of the police department. The police chief also mentioned a big party on the property? Is that something we need to talk about?"

Claire drew in a deep breath and struggled to answer calmly when everything in her wanted to throw something. "The only thing he could be talking about is that a lot of people came out to help me clean up after the storm. We built a big bonfire with all the fallen limbs. He wasn't at the party, but the next day he gave me a citation for having a bonfire without a permit."

The licensing worker nodded slowly. "Okay. I don't think this would be something that would keep you from being licensed, but I can't say it doesn't concern me that the police chief seems to be warning me off."

Claire struggled to maintain her dignity and not burst out crying. Even with the people going out of their way to support her, Roy had found a way to stir things up again.

Livvie looked up. "I almost forgot. What ages were you wanting to foster?"

"I was thinking older kids, or sibling groups, kids you might otherwise have trouble placing."

The social worker flipped her file closed and smiled. "Great. Got it. Hopefully, all this with the police chief will blow over, but maybe you should talk to him and see if you can set his mind at ease. I have high hopes for you and the children we will place here. Now, why don't you show me the barn and tell me about your plans out there before I head back to the office."

She took Livvie around the barn, introduced her to Freckles, who showed off, and to Tinkerbell, who definitely didn't. Tink's babies, though, were a huge hit. Nothing much cuter than baby goats. Especially ones who look angelic but were so spunky and mischievous.

She waved to Livvie as the licensing worker drove away, closed her eyes and drew in a deep breath. Done. One big step in her pages and pages of steps done.

Claire wasn't sure what to do about Roy, but it was clear that he wasn't going to drop his war on her. The only thing she could hope was that she had made enough friends that when it came time to vote in the town meeting that they would vote for her to stay.

Joe sat down at the kitchen table in Chap Campbell's house while the mayor himself poured Joe a cup of coffee.

Chap placed the cup in front of him with a little grimace. "I don't have too many visitors these days and since Margaret passed away last year, can't seem to be bothered with getting to the store much. I hope black is okay."

"It's fine, sir. I've been a cop for a dozen years. There's not much worse than station coffee." Joe took a big gulp of the coffee the mayor had put in front of him and almost took back his words. It was strong, hot and bitter. At least there was no danger of him falling asleep during this meeting.

Chap looked deep into his coffee mug and then said, "You must be wondering why I asked you to come out here this morning instead of meeting you at the Hilltop when Bertie's coffee has mine beat by a mile."

Joe didn't say anything, although he had wondered.

"I don't even know how to broach this subject, to be honest. Roy has been the acting chief since your dad passed away last year. I know he expects the title to be made official, but I'm not comfortable with that, especially after the way he treated your friend. I admit I bought into the fear he was trying to hype, but hopefully most everybody has seen through that now."

Again, Joe quietly waited. It was one of those skills he had learned while working as a negotiator. Sometimes waiting and watching was better than trying to control the situation.

Chap shook his head. "I don't want to step out of line and share things I shouldn't share about Roy. But I think we can do better for our little town. And I think we should."

"Have you asked other people to apply?"

"We sent a notice to other law enforcement agencies that we were looking. As you might guess, we haven't had a stellar response. A few résumés, no one that was qualified."

"All due respect, Chap, but what makes you think I'm qualified?"

"I did some research. Made some calls. Your CO—Todd?—made it very clear that he wasn't willing to lose you as a part of his team. But he couldn't help but tell me about your strengths as a leader and an officer."

He leaned forward. "Listen, Joe, what we have here is a diverse group of people who sometimes get crossways with each other and sometimes fail to understand each other's viewpoint. It's my opinion that a skilled negotiator could make a difference here."

Joe hesitated, forming his words carefully. "You make a good point, Chap. It's an idea worth some thought."

"We don't have a lot of crime here, but we're not naive enough to think that could never change." Chap swigged the last of his coffee and slammed his cup on a table scarred with stories of family life. "We want to keep our town a safe place for our citizens to live. We want to give the people who do live here a sense of community and pride. I think you can do that in a way that Roy never could. He is divisive and judgmental and that's just the truth."

"And you think I'm not...judgmental and divisive?"

"I think you've had to learn to understand other people's positions. And I think—and pardon my presumption here—that your background gives you a unique perception into *all* the people who live here in Red Hill Springs."

For as long as he could remember, Joe had wanted to escape his past in Red Hill Springs. He was having a hard time understanding that Chap considered his background a positive. The fact that he would even consider applying for the job seemed crazy. Thoughts buzzed in his head.

He was rejoining his team. He had a plan.

But his daughter was settled here.

And Claire.

He'd be lying to himself if he didn't admit that leaving her would be hard, and not just for Amelia. He would miss her list-making mania, her beautiful blue eyes and ever-present calming force in both his and Amelia's life.

Joe raised his eyes to meet Chap's shrewd gaze. "I'm really going to have to think this through and pray about it some. It's not just me that an offer like this affects."

Chap nodded. "You'll still have to go through

the town council and there might be a few on there who still remember your wilder days and one or two of them are tight with Roy. But I think they'll come around."

"Thank you, Chap. You've certainly given me a lot to think about." Joe shook Chap's hand and headed for his truck, sliding his sunglasses onto his face.

It was a tempting offer, but being a part of the crisis response team had been a dream for a long, long time. His team trained every day to take the calls no one else wanted to take. When other people were running away, his team ran into danger.

It was an adrenaline-pumping test of his intelligence and skill every day. Giving it up wouldn't be an easy decision. His team was depending on him and that was a hard thing to turn his back on.

Chapter Fifteen

❧

The door slammed open. "Claire!"

Silence before pint-size cowboy boots came stomping up the stairs. "Claire! We have a surprise for you!"

Claire stepped out into the hall from the second-floor girls' room, wiping her paint-stained fingers on the apron she'd started wearing for that purpose. "Calm down. You're going to burst a blood vessel if you keep that up."

Amelia put her hand on her hip and shot Claire a look.

Throwing her own multicolor hands up in surrender to a twelve-year-old's sass, Claire laughed. "Okay, okay. I'm coming, but only because it's almost time to quit for the day and I'm hungry."

"You're such a goober." At the bottom of

the stairs, Amelia stopped and whipped a bandanna out of her back pocket. "Blindfold."

"I don't think so, missy."

Amelia smiled sweetly. "Joe said you were too much of a control freak to wear it."

Claire stared into Amelia's shining eyes and wondered for the millionth time how a mother could have left this brilliant, feisty, beautiful child. "Fine, but only if you don't tell him I balked."

Amelia turned an imaginary key in her lips and mimed throwing it away. "Lips are sealed. Turn around."

While Amelia covered her eyes, Claire tried to pick her brain. "Is it chocolate?"

"No. Be still." Amelia pulled it tight, getting a piece of Claire's ponytail stuck in the knot.

"Oww!"

"Stop being a baby. Let's go." Amelia took her by the hand and led her down the long hall through the kitchen to the back door.

The cool breeze wafted across her face as Amelia opened the door.

"Wow, it feels good out here. Perfect weather." A dog barked in the distance and Claire groaned. "Please tell me you didn't get a puppy."

Amelia giggled. "Not a puppy."

Joe's rough, warm hand gripped her free one and her tummy did a crazy flip.

Crazy was right. She had already established in her traitorous little mind that the timing couldn't be worse for either of them.

Still. His hand felt so good, so right, in hers.

"A little farther. Watch the goat poop," Joe warned.

"How can I watch the goat poop when my eyes are covered?"

His laugh was a warm rolling chuckle in her ear. "I'm not sure, but it might've been too late for that warning. Almost there."

A high-pitched wheeze followed by a bellow cut through the yard. She stopped still, her mouth dropping open. "You didn't."

Joe laughed harder. "Take a look."

She whipped the bandanna off her face and in the pasture just beyond the fence, she saw the cutest gray-and-white donkey she'd ever seen. "It's a guard donkey. You guys!"

"She's really sweet, Claire. Her name is Radish." Amelia pulled a carrot out of her back pocket and handed it to Claire. "She likes carrots and apples, like Freckles."

Her new donkey had a fuzzy forehead and long white eyelashes. When she nipped Joe's hat off his head and trotted to the other side of the paddock, Claire fell hard.

Joe vaulted over the fence and chased the feisty donkey around the enclosure. He grabbed his hat and smushed it back on his head before walking over to where Amelia and Claire were standing. "She had me fooled. I thought she was docile."

The donkey shoved her head over the fence and nudged Claire until she got the other half of the carrot with her soft, fuzzy lips.

Claire put her free arm around Amelia and squeezed, but she was looking at Joe. "Thank you. She's really something special."

Joe grinned, lifting his hat and settling it again. "She's something, all right."

"Why don't you guys stay for dinner? I've got some hot dogs in the fridge and marshmallows left from the other night that really need to be roasted."

"Yes!" Amelia bounced in her boots, but Joe settled a hand on her shoulder.

"Homework."

Her face fell. "I only have a little."

His amused eyes met Claire's and she knew there was about to be a compromise. "How about I help Claire to feed the animals while you finish your homework? Then we'll all have dinner together."

An hour and a half later as the last of the light faded from the sky, Amelia slammed the back screen door open, a plate of hot dogs in one hand and a bunch of wire coat hangers in the other. "Are we going to use the hangers to cook the weenies?"

Claire tossed her gloves to Joe. "Why don't you get started unraveling those and we'll get those puppies started."

"We're grilling puppies? Eww!" He laughed as he took the coat hangers from Amelia.

Amelia rolled her eyes but smiled to herself as she brought the plate of hot dogs to the chairs by the fire. Claire couldn't help but think how far they had come in their relationship since their silent breakfast.

Joe unwound the coat hangers while Claire taught Amelia how to skewer the hot dogs. The first two fell on the ground.

"Ooh, Claire, I hope those don't bring out the coyotes." Amelia cackled at her own joke.

Claire laughed and looked over her shoulder toward the paddock. "Lucky me, I have a guard donkey named Radish. Those coyotes aren't going to come anywhere near me or my stock." She handed Amelia a completed one. "Now hold it over the fire pit until it starts to sizzle. When it's good and hot, that's when it's done."

Amelia squealed as her hot dog flamed up.

"Or just catch it on fire." Joe grinned as he pulled the hot dog out of the fire and blew it out. "Lucky for you guys, when I went to get my jacket from the cabin, I stuck one of Bertie's casseroles in the oven. It should be just about done."

Claire laughed. "Thank goodness. I'm starved!"

He started for the cabin and she watched him go, her smile fading as she realized she was starting to depend on a certain handsome cop who was planning to leave as soon as he got healthy.

Already she wasn't sure what she would do without him.

The fire had burned down to coals and Amelia was asleep in an Adirondack chair, wrapped in one of the quilts Claire had managed to salvage from the upstairs linen closet. Claire was snug against his side, quiet, watching the embers fly into the sky, tiny sparks of light. Country music played softly from a radio she'd set out on the back porch.

Joe stretched his legs toward the fire, his arm around her shoulders. He felt...at peace. It had been a long time since he felt anything like contentment and yet he found it here with Claire and Amelia in the middle of a barnyard with a donkey staring at him.

"The mayor asked me to apply for the job

of the chief of police." The words were out before he even knew he was going to say them.

"What? Wow! That's great! Right?"

"It's not something I ever thought about doing." He played with the ends of her hair, the silky strands sliding through his fingers. "All of this was a surprise to me."

She turned toward him. "All of this?"

"Amelia, the cabin..." His voice deepened further. "You."

Her eyes shimmered. Firelight gleamed gold. Her fresh scent wrapped around him, smoky and sweet She was so beautiful. He skimmed his fingers down her cheek and her eyes darted to his.

Her hand slid to his chest, her fingers spreading over his heart. "Your heart is so big, Joe. I knew it when you took one look at me and gave me your coffee the first morning I woke up here. Who shares their first cup of coffee?"

Joe didn't seem to be able to put two rational thoughts together in his head, but truth was he didn't want to. He wanted to stop thinking altogether and just be.

He lowered his lips to hers, drawing her closer. He wanted to drink in that sweetness, that irrepressible joy that was just her.

She clenched his shirt in her fist. He brushed his lips across hers. Once. Twice. Once more.

Then dropped his forehead against hers. "I don't know what to do, Claire."

She placed a tender kiss at the corner of his mouth and eased away from him so she could see his eyes. "Are you considering applying for the job?"

Right this minute, he was so conflicted. What he really wanted was to stay in this spot forever, with the fire crackling and the stars glimmering above them in the vast country sky. "All I ever wanted was to be on the tactical team. I worked hard for it."

"And your life here?"

His throat wanted to close around the words. "Frank and Bertie… I don't understand why they loved me, Claire. I was a total idiot all the time when I was a kid. I earned my way when I left here. I earned my place on the crisis response team. I don't want to walk away from it."

"I see." She didn't laugh. Her eyes, liquid pools of deep blue, searched his. She looked away and smoothed the flannel shirt under her palm. His heart gave a painful squeeze.

He tried to explain, but his feelings were a mixed-up jumble inside. He wasn't even sure how to make sense of them. "You mean so much to me, Claire. My life here with you and

Amelia on the farm. My family. I don't deserve it. I don't deserve for it to make me feel so…"

"Happy?"

"I guess, yes." He hadn't thought of it that way. But yes, maybe that was what he was feeling.

"You deserve to be happy, Joe. It's not something you have to earn."

Rationally, he got the concept. But the free gift of grace and love was something that had always just eluded his understanding. He shook his head. He'd been content with his work on the tactical team. Shouldn't that be enough?

"What about your daughter? Amelia just settled in here. Now you have someone else to think about besides just yourself."

"I know. I haven't stopped thinking about her. Staying means she wouldn't have to leave you, too. I need one of your lists of pros and cons."

"No. You don't. There are no lists that can tell you how to follow your heart. You're not a defenseless kid anymore, Joe. You have the power in this situation." She kissed him again, gently, making his heart ache. Longing. Loss. All mingled in together.

"I hope you figure it out." She walked into the house and closed the door, leaving him sitting in the dark.

* * *

Inside, Claire closed the kitchen door and fell back against it, sliding to the floor and burying her head in her hands. Maybe she should go out there and beg him to stay. It was what she wanted. Wasn't that the point, though? It was what *she* wanted. He had to make this decision for himself.

And when those feelings of being unwanted and unloved came roaring back, that was her stuff to deal with. He wasn't responsible for her issues.

She sighed. Being an adult was way harder than it should be.

She hauled her lousy self to the bedroom and flopped on the bed. When her cell phone buzzed in her back pocket, she rolled over to dig it out.

Jordan. Her family came through again. "Hey, sis. Please tell me you're finally on your way. I could really use a friend about now."

"What about the hot cop? I thought you guys were hitting it off."

Claire pulled the bedside table open and dug out a chocolate kiss. "We were—are. I don't know. I think he's planning to move back to Florida soon."

"He sounds stupid."

A laugh burst out. "He's not, but I love you. Thanks for being there for me."

"I'm going to be there in person in two days."

"I hope you're bringing a bed, because I have no furniture." The chocolate melting in her mouth and her sister on the other end of the call gave Claire some much-needed comfort.

"So needy." Jordan laughed and, in her mind, Claire could see her in flannel and jeans and boots, her feet propped up in front of the fire. "I can't wait to see the place."

"You're not going to recognize it. We're really doing this."

"We really are."

She could hear the sound of the road as Jordan drove down the highway and imagined her coming closer with every minute. "When Mom died, I was like, okay, now what am I going to do?"

"I know. I miss her every single second, but maybe it turned out okay in the end. We had to try to come up with our own life plan, or if you're me, hitch on to my sister's life plan."

"You're still doing your thing. You're just doing it here instead of there. Your horses are going to be a huge benefit to the kids who live here. The caseworker, Livvie, was super excited about it."

Silence for a second, then, "I'm really glad to hear you say that. I felt kind of like a second or third wheel, especially since I couldn't help with the reno."

"Don't worry. There's still plenty to do. Who do you think will plant the gardens?"

"Not it." Jordan paused. "Are you really okay? If Joe-Shmoe hurts you, I can totally sic Gus on him."

"I think siccing your German shepherd on him might be a little extreme, but I'm going to reserve that possibility." She laughed. "I really needed to talk to you. Thanks for that."

"Sisters gotta stick together. I'll see you in a couple of days and we'll eat a pint of ice cream and binge-watch some mindless television in our jammies."

"That sounds perfect. Keep me posted on where you are. I can't wait for you to get here." Claire hung up and stared at the little pile of silver wrappers she'd collected.

Her mom used to always sit her down at the kitchen table after she'd had a hard day and hand her a couple of chocolate kisses. Somehow in the unwrapping of the kisses, whatever was bothering her came unwrapped, too, emotions spilling out for her mom to hear. An argument with a friend, a boy who hurt her feelings. A bad grade. The sweetness of the chocolate combined with her mother's loving kindness always soothed the sting away.

So what would Mom say now? Something like, *Was your friendship with Joe your idea or God's?*

Claire sat with that awhile, thinking her mother was smarter than she was. *It was God's and mine, I thought.*

And then her mother would say, *If this was God, then it will work out no matter what you do. God is big enough to make this house a home for a dozen children and He is big enough to work your friendship with Joe out, too.*

But...

She'd always been stubborn, trying to argue with her mother's wisdom.

No, honey. We can't direct what we want God to do. We can only wait and be faithful in the meantime.

Waiting again. Tears stung her eyes. Her mother was right. This project was so labor-intensive—maybe she'd gotten the idea that it was all up to her to make it happen. It wasn't. It was all in God's hands from the start. Even Jordan. Even Amelia.

Even Joe.

She opened another kiss and stuffed it in her mouth. Mom always knew what to say and

Claire missed her with a physical ache, especially now when she was so close to realizing her dream. The kisses were just a reminder, but Claire supposed that was why she was so addicted to them now. They reminded her of love and a safe place.

Home.

The phone rang again. She rolled over and picked it up. Jordan always had one more thing to say. "What did you forget?"

There was a long pause. "Claire? This is Livvie Rabun, from Child Services."

Claire bolted upright. "Oh, hi. I'm so sorry. I just this second hung up the phone with my sister and thought it was her calling back."

Livvie laughed. "I'm hoping you're ready to fill that house up."

Her heart was jumping in her chest. She'd been waiting for this moment. Wasn't it too soon? How could she take in kids before her license was complete?

She didn't even have enough furniture! "Can you give me more information?"

"Spoken like a true veteran already. I know it's sooner than you expected, but we have a sibling group of four that's been separated and we'd really like to place them together. What do you say?"

Claire slowly sank back on the pillows. Four!

Have mercy. "How old? And when would they be coming?"

"They are…" She could hear papers shuffling. "Thirteen, eleven and nine-year-old twins." Silence stretched for a moment before Livvie said, "You have a little time. They're in other foster homes and they're safe. If you decide to take them, you can meet them whenever you like."

"Yes."

"What?" Livvie laughed again, her sunny personality coming through the phone. "I was all prepared to give you the hard sell."

Maybe God was making her wait because He had bigger plans for her. Sibling set of four—that was pretty big. Her mind was spinning, lists piling up already.

"Okay, try to get some sleep. It might be the last time you sleep for a while. I'll email you with more details tomorrow."

"Wait, Livvie. What about my license?"

"We'll have to have your background check back before we move them. I'll send you an email with the other foster parents' info so that you can get in touch and figure out details about transitioning them over."

The town council. She had to get the town council's approval, too. Maybe she didn't officially need it, but she wanted it. "Wait. Livvie."

The resource worker laughed. "Yes?"

"Is this a long-term or short-term placement?"

"We're always hoping for short-term. I don't have any real details on that right now, though."

"Okay, thanks." Claire hung up the phone, then picked it up again to call Jordan back.

Four kids. Whoa.

Chapter Sixteen

Claire couldn't stop smiling at her sister, Jordan, who had finally, *finally*, arrived at Red Hill Farm. They were getting the horses settled in the barn. They would turn them out to pasture in the morning after they had a night to get used to the new smells in Alabama.

Jordan hauled the water hose into the barn and filled four buckets. She added a scoop of fruit-flavored drink mix to each bucket so the horses wouldn't refuse water that didn't taste the same as they were used to, just like she had for the last couple of weeks in North Carolina.

Claire peeled a flake of hay for the small Arabian mare and double that for the bigger gelding quarter horses. She tossed the alfalfa hay into each stall and gave each horse a scratch on the neck. When Bartlet put his big gray head over the stall door, she whispered, "You'll get an apple in the morning, I promise."

"You're going to spoil them, aren't you?" Jordan was hanging each horse's halter and lead rope by the stall for easy access.

"Of course I am, right, Hagrid?" She loved the Haflinger pony, too, with his long blond mane, who bumped her with his broad face when she got close. She scratched between his fuzzy ears. "You goof, I missed you, too."

Jordan turned off the hose. "We all missed you. It was a long couple of months, especially knowing what you were going through down here with that crooked chief of police."

"I'm not sure he's crooked, just opinionated and judgy."

Her sister huffed and stepped into the stall with Leo, brushing him with quick, short strokes. A big brown horse with a white blaze on his face, he'd been Jordan's first therapy horse and would stand completely still to be groomed. "Whatever. That ticket for an unlicensed bonfire was ridiculous. As if people don't burn trash around here on a regular basis. I'm glad you had Joe here keeping an eye on you."

"I told you, Joe just lives here with his daughter." Claire grabbed a dandy brush out of a bucket. She opened Bartlet's stall door and nudged him out of the way so she could get in to groom him.

"And there's nothing between you except he's your tenant?"

"Exactly. And we're friends."

"Well, either you have yourself completely fooled or you're lying. Your voice changes when you talk about him."

"It does not!"

"Okay, then, tell me some things about Joe." Jordan paused midstroke. "What's he like as a father?"

An image popped into Claire's head: Joe and Amelia having a water fight while painting that crappy little cabin. The memory was sweet, the first time that she'd really seen them bonding. But it was the ache that came along with it that surprised her. She cleared her throat. "Um, he gets that he can't push her, that she responds better when they tackle projects together. He backs away when she needs space, but not so far that he's not there when she needs him."

"Sounds like a natural."

Claire smiled without thinking. "He is."

"What's his best characteristic?"

Steadfast. Honest. Loving. Thoughtful. "Okay, so maybe I think he's pretty great. That doesn't mean I'm in love with him."

Jordan, working by Leo's feet, didn't look up. "What does he look like? I've never seen him."

Claire pictured Joe, his silver aviators, pristine T-shirt, spotless jeans and those beat-up dirty boots. She chuckled. "Let's just say he can wear a pair of boots."

Jordan stood and draped her arm across Leo's back. "Do you not hear yourself? You're definitely in love with him."

"I'm not!" Claire's mind raced to find all the reasons that her sister was wrong. Except she couldn't think of a single one. Horrified tears sprang into her eyes. "I can't be."

"Why not?" Jordan stepped out of Leo's stall, closing the gate behind her and leaning over the door to Bartlet's stall. "Unless he's not a good guy."

"He is! He's…great." She shook her head. "He's amazing. He really is. But he's also leaving. He's said all along that he was going back to work in Florida as soon as he was healed."

"Then I guess you wouldn't have anything to lose." Jordan turned away as she started on Freckles. "Hey there, boy. Did you miss your barn buddies?"

Claire patted Bartlet's big rear as she moved around him to the other side. "What do you mean, I wouldn't have anything to lose?"

Jordan had witchy blue-green eyes instead

of the lake blue of Claire's, despite the fact that they were twins. Those knowing eyes peered out from under Freckles's neck. "I mean, if he's leaving anyway, you might as well tell him how you feel."

Claire rubbed the middle of her forehead where she could feel a headache starting. "Tell him what, exactly? I don't even know how I feel."

"You'll figure it out." Jordan squealed as Freckles pulled one of her braids between his velvety lips. "Let go of me, you naughty horse! Look, Claire, you know better than anyone that we're not promised tomorrow. Talk to him."

Jordan started brushing again with purpose. "You always want people to be straight with you. Be straight with him and then let him decide."

Claire bent over Bartlet's hoof to make sure he hadn't picked up a stone somewhere. A tiny pebble could get in there and make a big old horse lame if you weren't careful. Jordan had planted a thought in Claire's mind, and like a tiny pebble in a horse's hoof, it was going to worry her until she figured it out. She knew she really cared about Joe. She felt like there was potential for more, yes, but in love with him?

She couldn't be.

Right? Or had she just been lying to herself about her feelings for him? Neither one of them had a lot of margin for other things right now, but maybe Jordan was right.

Maybe she did owe it to herself to tell Joe the truth before he moved.

She tried out the words. *I'm in love with Joe Sheehan.*

Her heart began to pound in her chest, heat rushing her face as she recognized the truth she'd been dancing around for a long time.

God help me, I'm in love with Joe.

Joe bent over the instructions for the new set of twin beds Claire had ordered for the children who would be moving in here soon. He rolled his shoulder to ease the ache that still crept in from time to time. "I think it's that one."

Claire picked up a long straight piece and fit it into the slot in the headboard. "Yes! Okay, get the drill."

He drove the screw into the headboard. "Got it. Let's do the other side piece next."

"Already on it." Claire picked up the piece and Joe guided it into place. "It seems so strange that one day in the not too distant future, this house will be full of children."

"Your dream for Red Hill Farm is about to

come true." He drilled another long screw into the headboard and sat back on his heels. Claire didn't look like a force of nature, with her jeans and boots and long tunic T-shirt, but she most definitely was one. He'd never met anyone like her. "How does it feel?"

She flashed him a grin as she handed him the next screw. "Good. But I'll feel better when the town council gives me their approval. I know I can do this without them, but I don't want to."

He drilled the second screw into place. "I have a feeling you're going to be surprised that people are more supportive than you thought they would be."

"I hope so." Rolling to his feet, Joe picked up the footboard and held it while Claire whizzed the screws into place. "One down. You want to start on the next one?"

There was something soothing about working with his hands, seeing things take shape. He moved the headboard to the wall and looked around for Claire. She was still sitting in the same spot. "Claire?"

She looked down at her hands. "Actually, before we finish up here, there's something I've been wanting to talk to you about."

His heart rate kicked up. "Okay."

"I just...I know you're trying to make the

decision about whether to apply for chief of police or not. And when I make a decision, I like to have as much information as possible."

She stopped and looked down at her feet. He held his hand out to her, and when she slid her hand into his, he pulled her up.

Tugging her toward him, he held both of her hands. "Talk to me."

"I care about you, Joe. You came into my life at a time when I had no one and was teetering on the edge of losing it. And you didn't run away. Instead, you came back. With reinforcements. I don't know what I would've done without you and Bertie and Amelia."

He opened his mouth to respond, but she didn't give him a chance to talk.

"Amelia—I love that kid. She's resilient and funny and smart."

"She's amazing," he agreed. "But—"

"I don't want you to go, Joe. I want you to stay. For Amelia. And for Bertie." She paused, swallowing hard and looking away, out the window, like she'd rather be anywhere but here, having this conversation. "And for me. I want you to stay for me."

She pressed her fingers against his lips as he opened them to speak. "Let me get through what I have to say. I fell in love with you. I didn't mean to, but…I love you, Joe. In a totally improbable, unlikely, really unbelievable way. Seriously, I don't even believe it."

A weight settled into his stomach, a knot that he wasn't sure would ever go away. He didn't know what to say. He knew he had feelings for her. He'd spent enough time trying to shove them down. He hadn't even allowed himself to consider it.

Silence stretched.

"Okay." She took a step back. "Okay, I guess that settles that."

"It doesn't, Claire. It doesn't change how I feel about you that I can't declare those feelings at this exact moment. I need a minute. A month, maybe. I can't make promises when I don't know if I can keep them."

She drew in a breath and nodded. "That makes sense. I'm sorry if I overreacted. I feel like I'm laying my heart out on the floor and it's inevitable that it's going to get stomped on."

Joe took a step closer to her. The last thing he wanted was to hurt the person who meant the most to him. "I really hope that doesn't happen."

"You have the power, Luke Skywalker."

He laughed. She was so weird and perfect and he loved being with her. And he owed her the truth, or at least what he knew of the truth at this moment. "This afternoon I have an appointment with the specialist, and if I'm cleared for duty, I start training with my team next week."

The look of hurt on her face was quickly shuttered. She turned away from him to pick up the bed rail. "That's great, Joe. Really great. I'm glad that you're getting back to normal. What about Amelia?"

"I made an appointment with the principal of the middle school in my neighborhood. I'm touring it tomorrow." He heard a creak outside the door and turned to look, but no one was there and the sound didn't come again. He turned back to Claire. "The truth is that I'm not sure I'm making the right decision. And I'm not making the decision out of default, which is what would happen if I just keep putting it off."

"I understand, Joe. I really do."

She wasn't angry or even upset, so why did he feel so conflicted inside? He held the screw and drilled it into the bed rail. "Besides, it's not like any decision I make has to be forever."

"That's very true." She picked up another piece of the bed and held it in place. "I always told the teenagers I worked with, just because you make one bad decision, that doesn't mean you have to keep making them."

"Exactly." As he drilled the last screw into

place in the second single bed, he realized that Claire had taken his decision a lot more calmly than he would have. "Are you okay?"

She glanced up from where she was making the last few turns with a manual screwdriver. "Of course. Listen, I've got this from here. All I have left to do is put the cross-rails in and they are already cut and ready to go."

Joe held the drill in his hand and studied her face. She seemed okay. Maybe she just wanted him to leave. "Claire, I—"

She turned with a bright smile on her face. "You don't have to say anything else. I'm fine. You need to go."

After placing the drill on a piece of cardboard on the floor, he walked to the door and turned back. "Pensacola's not very far. I'll be back all the time for Amelia to see everyone. It's not like we won't stay in touch."

She straightened, her eyes serious. "No, I don't think so. I think if you go, it's best if we make a clean break."

"But—" When she didn't turn around, he let the word trail off. He wanted to force the issue, but honestly, he just didn't know what to say. "I guess I'll see you around, then."

She placed a cross-rail into the bed frame and screwed it into place without looking at him. "Okay, see ya."

* * *

"Promise me you won't forget me." Amelia whispered as she clamped her arms around Claire's waist.

"No way." She leaned back so she could see into Amelia's precious face. "You can come see me and the animals when you're here to visit Bertie."

"Why is Joe making me do this? I don't want to go, Claire."

Her emotions were all over the place, but even so, she knew she couldn't encourage Amelia not to trust Joe. "Honey, your dad made a promise to his team. Just promise me you'll give it some time."

Amelia buried her face in Claire's chest as Joe appeared in the door, those silver aviators concealing his expression. He cleared his throat. "Time to go, kiddo."

She backed up a step, out of Claire's arms, and scrubbed the tears off her face before whirling around and storming past Joe. A few seconds later, Claire heard the truck door slam.

Joe cleared his throat again. "She's, um, really thrilled about the new chapter in her life."

"Be patient with her. She was just getting settled. It's going to take time."

"I know." He hesitated, then stepped toward her. "Claire…"

She stepped back. "Don't, please."

His hands dropped to his sides. After two or three long seconds, he turned and left, closing the door behind him.

Claire walked to the kitchen sink, watching out the window as Joe's truck drove away, Amelia's bedroom furniture tied into the truck bed. She had a knot in her throat the size of Texas.

The refrigerator opened behind her and two spoons clanked onto the island. "Come on. Rocky road always helps."

She turned around. "It's nine thirty in the morning." But she took the spoon Jordan held out to her and dug it into the carton anyway. "He just seemed so clueless. Like he had no idea what in the world his leaving had to do with me."

Jordan spooned ice cream into her mouth and talked around it. "Men are idiots."

"That's accurate." Claire sat with the spoon in her mouth, except it wasn't that simple. She sighed. "He's not an idiot. He doesn't want to hurt me or Amelia. He just doesn't want to let his team down."

"That's actually kind of sweet."

"It is. He is. That kind of loyalty shouldn't be discounted. Right?" She took another bite of the ice cream. "Do you think I'm being dumb, getting so upset and hurt about this?"

"I think that last guy you went out with— the one that couldn't understand that you had a life outside of dating him—did a number on you. Not everyone is a selfish jerk, sometimes they're just kind of slow to figure things out."

Claire stopped with the spoon halfway to her mouth. "I was engaged to that jerk."

Jordan rolled her eyes toward the ceiling. "I know. Sometimes I really do question your judgment."

Claire opened her mouth to protest and closed it again. She had no argument there.

"Maybe don't write him off just yet. Give him a chance to do the right thing." Jordan dug into the ice cream again.

Claire put her spoon down on the island. "No. I have the kids to think about. In a couple of weeks, we're going to have four children and each one of them is going to be needing our attention. I don't have time for wishful thinking."

But as she went into the barn to feed the goats, her eyes filled with tears.

She missed them already.

Chapter Seventeen

A scant week later, Joe stood at the door to Claire's farmhouse, his heart slamming in his chest. How could a place that was so familiar seem so wrong? He turned to the barn, half expecting Amelia to come running out, hair bouncing, untied ribbon flying behind.

Instead, it was Claire standing in the open door, a wary expression on her beautiful face. And who could blame her? She'd asked him to stay away and he understood, but he needed her. Needed her help.

It wasn't how he'd imagined his homecoming. He stared at the black flashlight in his hand, thinking that dark would be here soon and he didn't know if Amelia had a light. Or a coat. The gnawing bite of fear in his stomach was relentless, reminding him over and over that he had failed.

He wanted to explain why he was here, but coherent words seemed too hard. "Amelia's gone."

Her posture was instantly alert. She stepped toward him. "What do you mean, gone?"

"She didn't come home from school, didn't *go* to school. I found out when she didn't get off the school bus. I managed to track her to the Greyhound station." He willed her to understand. "I know she got on a bus for Red Hill Springs. After that, I don't know. Mom hasn't seen her."

"I haven't seen her, but if she didn't want to be found, she'd know how to hide here. Have you checked the cabin?"

"No, I came straight to the house."

"Jordan!" Claire called. When her sister appeared, she quickly filled her in. "We'll start at the road and walk in and see if there's any sign she got dropped here."

Jordan nodded. "I'll search the barn from top to bottom and walk the pasture rails. Get a couple flashlights from the tack room. It's going to be dark soon."

Claire returned with a flashlight and started for the road. "Did you talk to her friends?"

"I don't think she has any in Pensacola." His voice cracked as he struggled to keep it together.

"What about here?"

"The ones I knew to ask." A flood of fear swamped him. He'd been her father for only a couple of months and there was still so much he didn't know. He folded, hands on his knees, trying to drag a breath into his constricted lungs. "I can't...if something happened to her..."

Her hand on his shoulder was comforting, but her words held a gentle command. "Come on. Let's start at the road. We'll do it together."

He nodded. "She was so miserable. I should've known. I should've done something before now."

Claire didn't respond; the only sound was her footfalls crunching on the oyster-shell drive. Their flashlights sent streaks of light ahead of them.

"I'm not seeing anything." He directed the light into the shadow of a huge magnolia tree. "Where did she go? She couldn't just vanish."

"I hate to even bring this up, but is it possible that her mother came looking for her?"

"She wouldn't go with her."

"I don't want to think so, either, but kids like Amelia always want to hope for the best. It's possible if her mother called that she would have responded."

"Kids like Amelia? I don't know what you

mean by that. She's a kid." He didn't want to hear this.

Her tone was kind. "I'm not saying she's not a great kid. She is. I'm saying that it's normal and natural for a kid to want to believe the best of her parent, even when past history suggests otherwise, especially when..."

Especially when they were impossibly unhappy where they were. Fantasies about the unstable parent as rescuer were a fact of life. He understood this, dealt with it all the time in his work and in his own past. Claire was trying to help. "I get it. I just don't want it to be true."

She stopped in the driveway and looked around. "I don't see any sign of her. She hid in the barn once before. If she's here, maybe she's hiding somewhere."

He checked his phone again to see if she'd called—she hadn't—and shoved the phone back in his pocket. "Maybe."

Jordan met them in the driveway, shaking her head. "I searched every inch of the barn from the loft down to the crib. She's not in there. I'm going to look around the pond and check the cabin, but if we don't find her, we need to think about calling in the authorities."

His temper shot through the roof. "I am the authorities. She's my responsibility."

Claire put a restraining hand on his arm and

he shook her off. He knew enough to know that this didn't look good. He knew his temper was driven by fear. He knew the longer Amelia was missing, the less chance they had of finding her.

He knew all that. But he didn't care. He just wanted her back.

"You're thinking like a father, not a cop. And I get that, but soon you're going to have to make some difficult decisions." Jordan turned and walked toward the pond, her flashlight illuminating the trees and path in front of her.

Joe dropped onto the picnic table bench and dragged his hand across his head, wrapping his arm around it as if he could block out the truth with that simple gesture.

He was lost.

Claire crouched in front of him and looked into his face.

"Did she say anything, give any indication that she was planning to run away?"

A knot rose in his throat, unwanted tears clouding his eyes. "No, but I knew she was really unhappy about being in Pensacola instead of here."

Her voice was quiet but calm. "Okay. There's one place we haven't looked and that's the house. Either Jordan or I was in it pretty much all day, but it's a big house with lots of small spaces. Let's do a thorough search, and then if Jordan doesn't find her or we don't find her, we'll call in the state police."

"All right." He stood but didn't move, barely able to breathe. "I can't lose her, Claire. I only just found her."

Without hesitating, she walked into his arms, wrapping hers around his waist, holding on. In spite of everything, she offered comfort. He pulled her to him, her soft curls against his chest. He let himself sink into the embrace, just for a second of peace.

Joe dragged in a breath and let her go. He had no right to hold on. "I'll start at the bottom and you start at the top and we'll meet halfway?"

"Okay."

Standing in the downstairs hall, he let the homey feel of the house soak in, listening to Claire's steps on the stairs.

He closed his eyes. "Dear God, I don't deserve Your help. I don't do what You say and I depend on myself way too much. But Amelia—Amelia's just a kid. My kid. And if anything happens to her, I won't survive it. Please, God, please keep her safe. Please let me find her."

He buried his face in his hands, unable to keep the quiet sobs from escaping. He'd let her down. In some indefinable way, he had been unable to be the father that she needed.

He felt a small hand touch his back. "Dad?"

Whirling around, he grabbed her up into his arms. "Oh, Amelia."

He lifted his head. "Claire, she's here! She's here."

Setting Amelia on the floor, he held her face in his hands. Tears streaked her cheeks, too. "Do you have any idea how scared we have been?"

Claire nearly tumbled down the stairs in her hurry to get to them. "Amelia?"

"She's fine. She's safe."

At this moment, he didn't care about anything except that she was right here in front of him, not cold or lost or kidnapped, where he couldn't get to her. As Claire pulled Amelia into a hug, he wrapped his arms around the two of them, holding on to the two most precious people in his life.

How had he ever thought he could live without them? Both of them. He'd gone back to his job because he believed everything he wanted was where he'd been.

He was so wrong.

Claire stepped back and mopped her tears with her shirttail. "Don't you scare me like that, again, ever. I can't take it."

"I'm sorry." Amelia, still tucked in at her father's side, nodded her head. "I promise I won't run away again."

Claire pulled her phone out and called Jordan. "We found her in the house." She paused. "Yep, under the stairs. I'm going to make them some hot chocolate." Another pause. "Yeah, okay, thanks."

She looked back at Joe. "Jordan's going to feed the rest of the animals before she comes in."

"Can I help? I really missed Tink and the babies." Amelia's eyes were big and dark, shadows still lingering there. Looking at her now, Joe didn't know how he could've ever thought it would be okay taking her from the home and security she'd found here.

"Go ahead. I'll be out in a few minutes. We'll stay at Gram's tonight."

He followed Claire into the kitchen, and while she stoked the fire, he sent a text to his mom: Found safe. "It's probably overprotective that I don't want to ever let her out of my sight again, isn't it?"

"Maybe a little."

When she stood, he grabbed her hands in his two. Her gaze locked with his and he saw regret there. When she started to back away, he stopped her. "Can I say something?"

She nodded, but the wariness hadn't left her eyes.

"I messed up. I thought everything would be okay because I was taking Amelia with me. What I didn't realize, or maybe didn't want to realize, was that I was leaving something really important here."

Her chin trembled and he wanted to stop right then and pull her into his arms, but he wanted—needed—her to hear what he'd discovered.

"I gave my notice today *before* I realized Amelia ran away. I just didn't have a chance to tell her. This is where Amelia feels safe and loved. And I get it, because it's where I feel safe and loved, too."

A lone tear slid down her cheek and he wiped it away with his thumb. "I love you, Claire. I really hope you'll give me a second chance."

His heart once again in his throat, he waited. She leaned forward, placing a sweet kiss on his lips. And she smiled, the light reaching all the way to her eyes. "Second chances are what this place was built for."

He wrapped his arms around her and lifted her off her feet. Her hands on either side of his face, she lowered her lips to his.

Finally, he was home.

* * *

Once again, Claire sat in the library community room, her fingers twisted together so hard her nails were white.

Beside her, Jordan had the end of her braid, twirling it. "This is horrible. Is this what it was like the first time you came to a meeting? It's like we're in court or something, waiting for a verdict, and half the town is here watching. I can't stand it."

Claire glanced at her. "I know. We've come a long way, though. Technically, we don't need their approval, but it would be a whole lot better if we had it."

Roy sat across the aisle from her at the far end of his row. Unlike the last time they were here, Roy sat alone. His face was expressionless.

The room quieted as the mayor walked to the podium and called the meeting to order and the nerves jumping in her stomach intensified.

Chap Campbell cleared his throat. "Thanks, everyone, for coming out tonight. We started this discussion a couple of months ago. One of our law enforcement officers had some concerns about potential problems with a foster home for difficult-to-place children. Claire, why don't you come up here?"

When she didn't move, Jordan elbowed her. "Go. Get up there. Represent."

She stood and made her way to stand beside the mayor. Smoothing her skirt with damp palms, she smiled nervously. It was silly. She knew these people. No longer was she a stranger, but she was a part of their lives and they a part of hers. They had survived a near-miss natural disaster together and had grown closer as they supported each other through it. She lifted her head and met Bertie's gaze. To her surprise, Bertie's eyes were shining with tears.

The mayor put his hand on Claire's shoulder. "Now, I will admit that I had no real understanding of what Claire here was planning to do when we first had the discussion about turning Red Hill Farm into a foster home. Since then I've had the opportunity to talk with Claire. I attended a listening session she had after church and I can say without reservation that I am in full support of Red Hill Farm being a family home for children who don't otherwise have one."

He shifted on his feet, looking down at them before returning his gaze to the crowded room. "To tell you the truth, I'm a little ashamed that I thought of what was comfortable for me and my town before I realized these are actual children we are talking about. So—" he reached into his suit coat pocket and pulled out a chocolate kiss "—I hereby cast my vote for Claire and Red Hill Farm."

He dropped the kiss into a glass bowl on the table in front of her and walked to his seat in the front row. Claire's breath caught. She stared at the silver-wrapped kiss.

Finally, she searched out the mayor, the question unspoken. He caught her eye and winked. The moment stretched, but it couldn't have been more than a few seconds before Jamie stood. Her son with autism had fallen in love with Freckles and Claire was pretty sure the feeling was mutual.

Jamie walked to the front of the room, a broad smile on her face. "I vote to have therapy with horses for children who need it."

She tossed a kiss into the bowl in front of Claire and whispered, "I don't know what we did before you came."

Bertie followed, placing her chocolate kiss in the bowl with the others. "I vote for all children to have a home where they will be loved and supported."

Claire's chest ached with the effort to keep it together.

A beautiful blonde with a little boy around six holding her hand walked to the front. She said, "I'm Harvey Haney's daughter, Mary Pat. I cast my vote for neighbors helping neighbors."

When she nudged him, her son tossed a kiss into the bowl and smiled at Claire, charming her with his missing two front teeth.

Claire choked back tears as Ellen walked forward. Ash. Lanna and Jules. Pastor Blakely. One by one, they cast their vote for Red Hill Farm. The bowl was brimming with chocolate kisses, the little silver wrappers shining in the warm light of the community room.

Those little kisses told her that she had been heard. That the community—her community—had listened. To her, like those long-ago afternoon chats with her mom, they were a symbol of burdens lifted and feelings safely shared.

She brushed dampness away from her eyes as Jordan came forward, a kiss in her hand, a wide grin on her face. "I vote for partnership and Red Hill Farm."

Amelia came next, a chocolate kiss in her hand. Her eyes were still a little uncertain, but she smiled when she dropped the kiss into the bowl. "I vote for family."

Claire grabbed Amelia in a hug, her eyes squeezed shut. When she opened them again,

Joe stood in front of her. She barely registered Amelia slipping back to her seat.

His sunglasses were nowhere to be seen and his piercing blue eyes seemed to see right into her soul. The corner of his mouth tugged up into a smile and she had to remind herself to breathe when he began to talk.

"I wasn't sure what to expect when I found you on the front porch at the old plantation home. Other people would have melted into hysterics at the condition of the place, but not you, Claire. You imagined children dancing, music playing." His eyebrows drew together in real consternation. "You have a knack of seeing beauty and potential in things that are scarred and broken.

"Even me. You showed me that I could make my life into whatever I wanted it to be. And I don't have to do it alone."

He reached into his pocket. She knew she would see a chocolate kiss. Her heart felt so full and so fragile, like it could shatter into a million pieces with a touch.

When he pulled his hand out, there in his palm lay a sparkling diamond solitaire with a little white tag, just like the candies.

She gasped, her gaze riveted on the ring.

Joe cleared his throat, and when he spoke again, his voice was raspy with emotion. "I want to spend the rest of my life with you. I want the bajillion kids who could come through our house and I want to love them all. I want forty-two horses and a dozen dogs and a family of goats. I want Amelia to have sisters and brothers. A whole ton of 'em. I want our holidays to be overrun with kids, with sleeping bags all over the floor because we have to cram to fit everyone under one roof. I love you, Claire. Please, marry me."

Claire stared at the ring in his hand. She'd come here to give foster kids a second chance, a new life. Well, standing right here in front of her was hers.

She looked into his perfect blue eyes and smiled.

"Yes."

Epilogue

"Is she here yet?" Joe slammed the door of his official police vehicle and strode to where Claire was sitting on the picnic table in the warm April sun, her tablet in hand, making a list. With seven children, she didn't have time to be looking for notes she wrote randomly to herself all day.

He leaned over, and when she looked up with a distracted smile, he dropped a kiss on her lips.

Her eyes lit up, her arm snaking around his neck to pull him in for another. "I missed you."

He growled in the back of his throat and pulled her closer. "I missed you more."

"Is she here yet?" Jordan swung her legs over the fence and dropped to the ground. "Seriously, guys? Is this the right time to be kissing?"

Joe grinned. "Is there a bad time for kissing?"

A door slammed open upstairs. "Mom, is she here yet?"

"Not yet, Amelia. Any minute."

Jordan started for the house. "I'll go check on the kids inside. Do you want me to order the pizza?"

"Yes, it's tradition now, so we have to." Claire looked up at Joe, a glint of humor in her eyes. "We're all a little excited."

"I hear ya. How's the list coming?"

"We moved Derio in with the younger guys so Kiera can have her own room. I went ahead and got the boys to put a crib in there, but I figured she would want to pick out the bedding and stuff herself."

"Did Mom take the kids to the store?"

"Yes, each of the kids picked their item for the welcome basket. We have peanut butter crackers, a stuffed animal, a pair of fuzzy socks, a Hershey bar, an iTunes gift card, a bottle of vitamins and some ear plugs."

He snorted a laugh. "Ear plugs?"

"Apparently, Crystal thinks our house is louder than the juvenile facility she came here from. I added a monogrammed backpack like the other girls have, so that leaves you."

He reached in his pocket and pulled out a familiar velvet box. Inside was a round charm engraved with today's date on a simple gold chain. The start of a new life. No matter what she chose to do with it, Kiera would have this reminder that today she had a second chance.

Joe knew about those, thanks to Claire. He pulled another box out of his other pocket, this one with a single pearl. Claire had one for each of the children who had become a part of their family over the last few months.

Her eyes held a suspicious shine and he pulled her closer again. He loved that she was already invested in a child she hadn't even met. "It's gonna be okay, sweetheart."

"I have one for you, too." She pulled a slim box from her bag.

"What is this?" He gave it a surreptitious shake.

"Open it."

Taking the top off, he found a thin stick with a small screen with one word on it. *Pregnant.*

His head whipped up. "You. We… Wait." He looked at the stick again. "We're having a baby?"

She nodded, eyes brimming now.

Joe let out a whoop and swung her off the table and into his arms, nuzzling her neck and making her squirm before setting her on her feet. "A baby? It's just… Wow. Wow."

"Do you think we're crazy?" She laughed, but her voice held a hint of vulnerability. He laced his fingers with hers as the caseworker's car turned into the drive.

Children and teens seemed to come pouring out of everywhere, including the twin ten-year-olds who came running from the barn, followed by a frolicking set of goat twins.

Joe laughed and pressed a kiss into her hair. "Definitely crazy. In the best possible way."

When Kiera got out of the car, he watched as the family—his family—welcomed her. Against all odds, they'd actually managed to turn this old place into a home.

In real life, second chances didn't come along every day. But here at Red Hill Farm, they did.

* * * * *

If you enjoyed THE DAD NEXT DOOR,
look for these other
emotionally gripping stories:

THE RANCHER'S TEXAS MATCH
by Brenda Minton

LONE STAR DAD
by Linda Goodnight

And the rest of the FAMILY BLESSINGS
miniseries by Stephanie Dees,
coming soon from Love Inspired!

Find more great reads at
www.LoveInspired.com

A door slammed open upstairs. "Mom, is she here yet?"

"Not yet, Amelia. Any minute."

Jordan started for the house. "I'll go check on the kids inside. Do you want me to order the pizza?"

"Yes, it's tradition now, so we have to." Claire looked up at Joe, a glint of humor in her eyes. "We're all a little excited."

"I hear ya. How's the list coming?"

"We moved Derio in with the younger guys so Kiera can have her own room. I went ahead and got the boys to put a crib in there, but I figured she would want to pick out the bedding and stuff herself."

"Did Mom take the kids to the store?"

"Yes, each of the kids picked their item for the welcome basket. We have peanut butter crackers, a stuffed animal, a pair of fuzzy socks, a Hershey bar, an iTunes gift card, a bottle of vitamins and some ear plugs."

He snorted a laugh. "Ear plugs?"

"Apparently, Crystal thinks our house is louder than the juvenile facility she came here from. I added a monogrammed backpack like the other girls have, so that leaves you."

He reached in his pocket and pulled out a familiar velvet box. Inside was a round charm engraved with today's date on a simple gold chain. The start of a new life. No matter what she chose to do with it, Kiera would have this reminder that today she had a second chance.

Joe knew about those, thanks to Claire. He pulled another box out of his other pocket, this one with a single pearl. Claire had one for each of the children who had become a part of their family over the last few months.

Her eyes held a suspicious shine and he pulled her closer again. He loved that she was already invested in a child she hadn't even met. "It's gonna be okay, sweetheart."

"I have one for you, too." She pulled a slim box from her bag.

"What is this?" He gave it a surreptitious shake.

"Open it."

Taking the top off, he found a thin stick with a small screen with one word on it. *Pregnant.*

His head whipped up. "You. We... Wait." He looked at the stick again. "We're having a baby?"

She nodded, eyes brimming now.

Joe let out a whoop and swung her off the table and into his arms, nuzzling her neck and making her squirm before setting her on her feet. "A baby? It's just... Wow. Wow."

"Do you think we're crazy?" She laughed, but her voice held a hint of vulnerability. He

Dear Reader,

Thanks so much for spending some time in Red Hill Springs, Alabama! The name of my fictional small town is inspired by real-life springs, where the waters have been flowing—and providing respite and relief for weary travelers—for hundreds of years.

Each of the Sheehan siblings is facing challenges, but through faith and with love, they will learn that sometimes broken dreams lead to family blessings. If you liked *The Dad Next Door*, please join me back in Red Hill Springs in October for the next book in the Family Blessings series.

I'd love to hear from you! I can be reached at my website, stephaniedees.com, or via email at steph@stephaniedees.com.

Stephanie Dees

Get 2 Free Books,
Plus 2 Free Gifts—
just for trying the
Reader Service!

LIS17R

Get 2 Free Books,
Plus 2 Free Gifts—
just for trying the Reader Service!

HARLEQUIN
HEARTWARMING™

HOMETOWN HEARTS ♡

YES! Please send me **The Hometown Hearts Collection** in Larger Print. This collection begins with 3 FREE books and 2 FREE gifts in the first shipment. Along with my 3 free books, I'll also get the next 4 books from the Hometown Hearts Collection, in LARGER PRINT, which I may either return and owe nothing, or keep for the low price of $4.99 U.S./ $5.89 CDN each plus $2.99 for shipping and handling per shipment*. If I decide to continue, about once a month for 8 months I will get 6 or 7 more books, but will only need to pay for 4. That means 2 or 3 books in every shipment will be FREE! If I decide to keep the entire collection, I'll have paid for only 32 books because 19 books are FREE! I understand that accepting the 3 free books and gifts places me under no obligation to buy anything. I can always return a shipment and cancel at any time. My free books and gifts are mine to keep no matter what I decide.

262 HCN 3432 462 HCN 3432

Name	(PLEASE PRINT)	
Address		Apt. #
City	State/Prov.	Zip/Postal Code

Signature (if under 18, a parent or guardian must sign)

Mail to the **Reader Service:**
IN U.S.A.: P.O. Box 1867, Buffalo, NY. 14240-1867
IN CANADA: P.O. Box 609, Fort Erie, Ontario L2A 5X3

* Terms and prices subject to change without notice. Prices do not include applicable taxes. Sales tax applicable in NY. Canadian residents will be charged applicable taxes. This offer is limited to one order per household. All orders subject to approval. Credit or debit balances in a customer's account(s) may be offset by any other outstanding balance owed by or to the customer. Please allow 4 to 6 weeks for delivery. Offer available while quantities last. Offer not available to Quebec residents.

Your Privacy—The Reader Service is committed to protecting your privacy. Our Privacy Policy is available online at www.ReaderService.com or upon request from the Reader Service.

We make a portion of our mailing list available to reputable third parties that offer products we believe may interest you. If you prefer that we not exchange your name with third parties, or if you wish to clarify or modify your communication preferences, please visit us at www.ReaderService.com/consumerschoice or write to us at Reader Service Preference Service, P.O. Box 9062, Buffalo, NY. 14240-9062. Include your complete name and address.